BRIDE REQUIRED

BY
ALISON FRASER

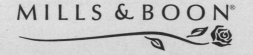
MILLS & BOON®

First published in Great Britain 1997
Harlequin Mills & Boon Limited,
Eton House, 18-24 Paradise Road, Richmond, Surrey TW9 1SR

© Alison Fraser 1997

ISBN 0 263 80605 7

Set in Times Roman 10 on 10¼ pt.
01-9802-59050 C1

Printed and bound in Great Britain
by Mackays of Chatham PLC, Chatham

'I assume you're single, too?'

'Single?'

'As in unmarried.'

'Of course.' Dee laughed. 'Why?'

Baxter hesitated, then finally decided to get round to the reason he'd approached her.

He grimaced before relaying the information. 'You can't be married because that's part of the job—getting married.'

Getting married? Dee repeated the words to herself, as if by doing so they might take on a new meaning, but they didn't. Then she took to staring at him as if he were completely and utterly mad.

He wanted her to marry him and she didn't even know his name!

Alison Fraser was born and brought up in the far north of Scotland. She studied English literature at university and taught maths for a while, then became a computer programmer. She took up writing as a hobby and it is still very much so, in that she doesn't take it too seriously! Alison has two dogs, two young children but only one husband. She currently lives in West Lothian and is in her early forties—she doesn't know what she wants to be when she grows up!

CHAPTER ONE

BAXTER was just about to give up the search when he found the right girl.

She was sitting in a long corridor that connected underground platforms. He looked for the usual cardboard sign saying 'hungry and homeless'. There wasn't one. She sat, eyes on the ground, playing a flute, and left passers-by to choose whether to throw a coin in her instrument case or not.

But she was still one of them: the dispossessed, the destitute, the growing army of young people living on the streets. It might have shocked him, their number—it was such a contrast to the affluence of central London—but he'd been warned that the capital had changed in ten years. And, besides, he'd seen worse on the streets of Addis and Mogotu.

Later he was to question why he'd selected her. At the time it was first impressions. She was wearing an army-surplus jacket and torn jeans, but at least they looked reasonably clean. She was young, but not too young. The flute playing put her one up the scale from begging, but still suggested she might be desperate enough.

Or perhaps it was simply the dog.

He'd seen several homeless people with dogs. Mostly men or couples, New Age travellers—whatever they were—with some scrawny animal, perhaps in the hope of eliciting more sympathy than their merely human plight. But they'd been mongrels, dogs cast on the streets like their owners.

This girl's dog was something else—a pure-bred retriever with a healthy coat and benign disposition; he barely opened a sleepy eye at the world passing by.

The girl didn't look up either, even when he drew near and threw a pound coin in the case. She might have nodded in acknowledgement of the offering, but her eyes remained fixed on the ground while her fingers continued to scale the instrument.

Baxter walked along, stopping only when he'd turned a corner. He was in two minds. He hadn't really caught a good look at her face, but what he'd seen of her—hair cropped short, and the three gold rings adorning one ear-lobe—wasn't exactly to his taste. She wasn't the sort of girl he would have dated, but that was scarcely relevant. At least she didn't look as if she might do nightshift as a hooker, which was more than could be said for some of the girls he'd considered that day.

He rehearsed what he was going to say before retracing his steps and coming to a halt before her.

Dee had a good memory for shoes. After all what else did she stare at all day? You didn't stare at the punters. They were nobody. Start looking at them and they might think they were somebody. Terry had told her that. He worked a pitch on the Northern Line, playing a guitar—badly.

So it was the shoes she recognised. Brown laced boots of the walking kind. They had passed five minutes earlier, dropping a pound in her flute case. Now they were back, and she didn't think it was to admire her virtuoso performance.

She resisted taking a squint at their owner, and kept playing. It had happened before. Guys who fancied their chances. Guys who imagined she might like to make more money flat on her back. She kept playing, but this one stood where he was, waiting for her to acknowledge him.

When she finally looked up, she was surprised.

She'd expected some creepy-looking individual, and instead registered a tall man with brown hair streaked blond by an un-English sun, straight brows and an angular face that could have belonged to a male model.

The handsome face creased into an equally handsome smile that had Dee muttering 'Phoney,' to herself even before he spoke.

'You're very good.' He nodded towards the flute.

'I know,' she responded, unimpressed.

He was disconcerted for a moment, then murmured dryly, 'Not hampered by false modesty, either.'

She shrugged, dismissing his opinion, then, raising her flute back to her lips, waited for him to move on.

It was a heavy enough hint, but he chose to ignore it.

She decided an even heavier one was required. 'Look, mate, I have a living to earn, so, unless you're a talent scout for the London Philharmonic...'

'Unfortunately, no.' He briefly flashed straight white teeth at her in a smile that never reached his eyes. 'I do have another proposition for you, however.'

'I bet,' Dee muttered darkly in return.

'Not that kind.' He was quick to correct any wrong impressions.

Dee continued to look at him sceptically, but then she looked at all men that way now.

'Look—' he took out his wallet and produced a twenty-pound note '—I'll pay for your time.'

'You *do* think I'm cheap, don't you?' Dee wasn't sure what the going rate for an afternoon quickie was, but she felt it should be more than that.

His eyes narrowed, displaying the first trace of anger. 'I just want to talk to you. Nothing sexual. Believe me.'

The reassurance rang true, as did his glance, which travelled over her asexual clothing, thin, pallid face and cropped hair. Whatever this man wanted, it wasn't her body.

Dee should have been pleased. She dressed this way specifically *not* to attract the opposite sex. But to have someone look at her quite so dismissively was offensive.

'We can go to the nearest café and I'll buy you and Rover a tea.' His glance was warmer when it was directed at the dog.

'Henry.'

'Pardon?'

'That's his name,' Dee informed him, wondering why she had.

'Henry,' he repeated, and put out a hand as the dog

slowly lifted himself to a sitting position so he could be petted.

Dee watched as the stranger stroked her dog on the head and scratched him in exactly the right position behind his ears.

'Sucker,' she muttered to herself as the dog responded by licking the man's hand and spoiled any chance of her claiming him to be fierce. Right from a puppy, he had been a slave for affection.

'Henry!' She glared at the dog until he subsided on stiff back legs.

'How old is he? Eleven? Twelve?' The man judged the dog by his movement.

'Thirteen.' Her eyes shaded with sad thoughts; it was a brief lapse before she added, 'His teeth are still sharp enough.'

'I'm sure they are,' he conceded, but there was a definite smile in his voice. He knew dogs and realised this one was as likely to bite him as he was to win a greyhound derby. 'He looks very mean and hungry.'

Dee understood it as sarcasm but chose to take it literally. 'He's never hungry! He gets fed fine.'

She glared at him as if he were an RSPCA inspector.

'I can see that.' His eyes travelled over the dog's rounded flank, then switched their scrutiny to her. 'It's you who looks like you could do with a meal or two.'

'Thanks.' Dee pulled a face, recognising an insult when she heard one.

Nonetheless he was right. She skipped meals—sometimes because she had no option—and it showed.

He upped the price. 'Thirty pounds, and you and Henry, here, can dine like royalty tonight.'

Thirty pounds was hard to resist. But Dee wasn't a fool.

'You're going to give me thirty quid just to sit in a café and talk...?' Stroll on, mate.' Her tone was hard with disbelief.

Baxter didn't blame her. He was beginning to think it a crazy idea himself. But, now he'd come this far and actually approached a girl, he had nothing to lose.

'As I said, I have a proposition...call it a job if you like,' he went on. 'Unusual rather than dangerous, and emphatically not of a sexual nature... I'm not interested in young girls,' he added on an unequivocal note.

That figures, Dee thought, admitting to herself—now that it was safe—that she had found him passingly attractive.

'I read you.' She defrosted a little to a fellow underdog.

'I doubt it,' he replied dryly.

'Makes no odds to me, mate,' she assured him. 'Live and let live is my motto.'

'Look, that's not...' About to correct any wrong impressions, Baxter decided not to bother. Why not leave her thinking it, if it was to his advantage?

'Right, I choose the café,' she suddenly conceded as she began to collect up her earnings and box her flute.

'Right,' he echoed.

She stood before adding, 'Money up front, of course.'

Baxter looked at her outstretched hand, his eyes narrowing in distrust. If he gave her the money now, what was to stop her making a run for it?

He hesitated too long.

'Forget it, then.' She made to walk away.

He caught her arm. Not roughly, just to stop her. 'All right. Half now, and half when we've talked.'

'Yeah, okay.' Fifteen pounds was better than nothing if she decided to give him the slip, Dee considered.

Only he was thinking ahead of her. When he said half, he meant half. She watched him tear a twenty- and a ten-pound note down the middle and present her with the two halves.

Dee grimaced but took the money, and, shouldering her rucksack, picked up Henry's lead.

Baxter noticed how laden she was. 'I'll take that.' He relieved her of the flute case before she could protest. 'And the rucksack if you like.'

'Don't bother.' Dee could have read it as a gentlemanly gesture, but didn't. 'You have enough insurance with my flute.'

Insurance against her running away, she meant.

Baxter raised a brow. 'Such scepticism in one so young... How young, by the way?' For an awful moment he wondered if she might be *too* young. Who knew with these runaways? She talked as though she were thirty and her eyes were old with knowledge, but her skin was un-lined.

'How old do I have to be?' she countered, suspicious again.

Baxter avoided a direct answer, and said, 'Old enough to have a job.'

He could hardly say sixteen—the age of consent.

'Yeah, well, I'm that all right.' Only she couldn't get one. The recession meant jobs were scarce for most young people—and non-existent for the homeless.

'Good.' Baxter nodded in relief and fell in step beside her as she took the steps down to the eastbound platform.

He considered making conversation with her, but her profile didn't invite any. She was unusually self-contained for a young girl. Was that good or bad for his purpose? Good, maybe. Less likely to be indiscreet.

Dee, for her part, was quite aware of the stranger beside her. She could hardly not be. She had always been tall. It had caused her untold agonies as a child. At sixteen she'd been five feet eleven inches and had thought she might go on growing for ever, but then, thank God, she had suddenly stopped. Still, she towered over most people. But not this man.

She was glad when a blast of cold air heralded the arrival of the tube. They boarded together and went through five stops in silence until they reached Newhouse station.

It was only when they approached the ticket collector that she confessed, 'By the way, I haven't got a ticket.'

'Great, a fare dodger,' he said in exasperation. 'I should have known.'

What should he have known? That girls like her had to be dishonest? Dee glared at him.

'You know nothing,' she responded. It was an accusa-tion, and they exchanged hostile looks for a moment, before she thrust Henry's lead at him. 'Don't worry about it. You take him. We'll meet up outside.'

'Hold on, wait a—' He didn't get the chance to finish.

He watched, with a mixture of horror and fascination, as

she veered towards the closed booth next door and leapt over the metal barrier.

He thought she was home free, but the collector caught a glimpse of her flashing past and sent a shout up.

The dog shot forward, too. Baxter found himself making excuses as they queue-jumped, and emerged from the barriers in time to see two underground officials restraining the girl.

He could have walked away. He might have if he hadn't still been attached to a dog who was suddenly barking with surprising ferocity at the guards holding his mistress's arms. So much for discretion.

Quick at thinking on his feet, Baxter took the initiative. 'I suppose you think that was funny?' He addressed the scolding comment to the girl before speaking to the guards. 'Kids these days, and their idea of fun! I'm awfully sorry about this—'

'You know her?' one of the men interrupted.

'I wish I could deny it,' Baxter ran on, 'but, yes, believe it or not, this scruffy urchin is my niece, Morag.'

Both officials were silent for a moment, deciding whether they should believe it or not.

So was Dee. *Morag?* What kind of name was that?

'She had a ticket but lost it.' He seemed to lie with ease. 'I was, of course, going to buy another at the exit, but the silly girl decided to leap the barriers instead. I believe it's the latest craze among teenagers. Slightly safer, I suppose, than playing chicken on the motorway.'

'But more expensive,' the second guard stated, unmoved. 'I'm afraid if you're going to ask us to let her off, sir, you're going to be disappointed. London Underground have initiated a drive to catch fare dodgers, with the intention of fining them.'

'Well, I don't blame you,' Baxter returned, which made Dee wonder whose side he was on. 'You've been a very silly girl. What's your mother going to say?'

'I don't know,' Dee mumbled, not sure of her words in this play, but realising she should at least act contrite.

He shook his head at her and asked of his fellow grown-ups, 'What can you do with them? It'll break her mother's heart... What now...? An on-the-spot fine?'

The first guard weakened. 'Well, I suppose if you were to pay the maximum fare possible for your route, then that might be acceptable.'

He looked to his colleague, who in turn stared at Dee as if he really would have preferred to hang, draw and quarter her, but then gave way with a shrug. Perhaps it was just too much bother at the end of a long day.

'Thank you very much.' Baxter shook both men's hands in gratitude as they released Dee. 'What do you say, Morag?' he prompted her.

'I...yes, thanks,' she trotted out dutifully, feeling five years old.

'Right. Take Henry.' He handed her back the dog and asked of the guard, 'How much do we owe you?'

'I'll find out.'

One guard went to the ticket office while the other remained with them.

Dee waited till he glanced away for a moment, and mouthed at her 'uncle', 'We could run.'

It drew a black look and a terse but distinct, 'Forget it,' in return.

Dee still could have run but it didn't seem a very honourable thing to abandon him after he'd rescued her. So she waited with him, and just stopped herself from making a rude comment when they were asked for some exorbitant sum—much more than five stops on the tube—to cover her misdemeanour.

The stranger took out his wallet once more and paid it without quibbling.

As they finally emerged into daylight Dee fought a battle with herself. She knew she should thank him for what he'd done, but she resented it as well. It put her in his debt, and she hated that.

'Normally it's no problem. They've barely enough staff to collect the tickets.' She justified what now seemed a silly action on her part. 'Anyway, you should have just left it.'

'And let them cart you off to jail?' He reminded her of the alternative.

'It wouldn't have come to that,' she told him knowingly. 'Even if they'd called the railway police, what were they going to do? Take my name and the address I haven't got? Fine me money I don't have? Big deal!'

He shook his head at her streetwise reasoning, then remarked dryly, 'Such gratitude, quite overwhelming.'

At this, Dee had sufficient grace to concede, 'Yeah, okay, I suppose I should thank you.'

'Not if it's going to kill you.' He dismissed the subject, and added, 'Which way to this café?'

Dee had almost forgotten where they were meant to be going. She considered giving him the slip, but now it seemed tantamount to stealing. He'd already half-paid her, and shelled out for her penalty fare. The least she could do was sit in a café and listen for five minutes.

'This way.' She let him fall in beside her. 'It's not far.'

She led the way off the main thoroughfare to a backstreet café. On occasion she washed dishes for the owner. In return, he gave her a couple of quid and let her sit with Henry and nurse a tea for an hour or so in cold weather.

Rick, the owner, eyed her companion for a moment when they entered, then asked,'Everything okay, Dee?'

'Sure.' She returned his smile with a brief one of her own. 'Could we have a couple of teas?'

Rick nodded. 'I'll bring them over.'

'Dee?' he repeated as they sat in the corner. 'That's your name?'

She nodded. Dee was the shortened version. Deborah DeCourcy was just too distinctive to go broadcasting.

She realised Dee probably sounded common to him, and muttered back, 'Better than *Morag,* at any rate. What made you pick that?'

'I've found that if you have to tell lies, it's best to keep them to the minimum,' he returned. 'I *do* have a niece. She *is* called Morag. And her mother *would* be horrified if she took to fare dodging... But presumably it's your main means of transport,' he concluded with dry disapproval.

'Actually, no, I normally walk,' she claimed, quite truthfully. 'As you might appreciate, it's hard to keep a low profile, leaping barriers with a large dog in tandem.'

Baxter raised a brow. Not at the sarcasm, but at her use of English. Mostly she talked with an East End accent, but once in a while it slipped. Then she sounded pure Home Counties, and educated at that.

'You said you were homeless,' he recalled, 'so where do you and Henry sleep? A hostel?'

She shook her head. 'They don't allow dogs and, even if they did, there's no privacy.'

Baxter mentally raised another eyebrow. 'You've obviously not heard the expression, "beggars can't be choosers".'

He didn't expect her reaction; she rounded on him furiously. '*I am not a beggar!* I'm a busker. There is a difference!'

'Okay! Okay!' he pacified in quick order. 'I didn't mean anything by it.'

Her eyes still flashed with anger. Expressive eyes, blue and wide, and revealing a passionate nature behind the cool exterior. He studied her face properly for the first time and was surprised to discover it was more than passingly pretty.

Dee didn't like the way he was looking at her. In fact, she was contemplating telling him to stuff his money when Rick turned up with the teas.

'You want work Saturday afternoon?' he asked as he laid them down.

'Yeah, okay,' Dee shrugged, and Rick departed with a satisfied nod.

'You work here?'

'Sometimes, when Rick needs someone to wash dishes.'

'So we're on your home territory?' he pursued.

'Sort of...I live in a squat nearby.' She didn't go into specifics.

Baxter added, 'On your own?'

Her eyes narrowed. 'Is it relevant?'

They had returned to the suspicious phase of their relationship.

Baxter sighed. 'To me personally, no, but for this...job I have in mind, it's best that you're unattached.'

'Then I'm unattached,' she revealed, then added on impulse, 'What about you? Have you a significant other?'

The question took Baxter by surprise. He half smiled at the cheek of her, before saying, 'I don't think that's any of your business.'

'I'll take that as a ycs.' She helped herself to four sugars before she noticed his appalled stare. 'Got to get your calories any way you can.'

'With most women it's the other way round,' he commented dryly.

She pulled a face, then quipped, 'Maybe I should write a book, passing on tips. *The no home, no hips diet.* Live rough and watch the pounds fall off.'

Baxter laughed, although it wasn't really funny. Perhaps he had compassion fatigue. He'd spent much of the last decade in the Third World, where hunger meant death.

Pity stirred in him as he watched her drink down her tea with great thirst. 'What's the food like in this place?'

She gave a short laugh. 'Great, if you're into greasy-spoon cuisine and want a cholesterol level in double figures.'

'I see what you mean.' Baxter scanned a menu that boasted endless variations of something and chips. 'Still, I'll risk it if you will…my treat.'

Dee's pride told her to turn down charity, but her stomach was speaking a different language. 'I suppose I could keep you company.'

'Gracious of you,' he drawled at her offhand acceptance, then signalled to the owner.

He came over and asked without much interest, 'Problem, is there?'

'No, we'd like to order some food,' Baxter told him.

Rick looked put out, then said in a resigned tone, 'Yeah, okay.'

'Dee?' Baxter invited her to order first.

She hesitated, then decided that if she was going to take charity she might as well go the whole distance. 'Sausage, bacon, tomato, fried bread, egg and chips.'

Baxter just stopped himself raising a brow at this list and muttered, 'Twice.'

'Yeah, okay,' Rick said once more, sighing at the effort it was going to cost him to cook it.

'Cheery sort of fellow,' Baxter remarked when he was out of earshot.

Dee wasn't a great fan of Rick either, but she felt the need to defend him. 'His wife left him recently. He's still cut up about it. Cleaned out their bank account, too.'

'That's women for you,' Baxter joked, forgetting she was one for a moment.

Dee realised it and flipped back, 'Well, if it is, you don't have to worry.'

'Sorry?'

'About women.'

'Not being married, no,' he agreed.

'Nor likely to be either,' she added a little tartly.

Baxter assumed he was being insulted, but chose to laugh instead. 'You think I'm so ineligible?'

Dee frowned. 'Well, naturally, I assumed...unless, of course, you're bisexual.'

'*Bisexual?*' He looked at her as if she were mad.

'Okay, okay, just a suggestion.' She held her hands up, taking it back. 'Is that some sort of insult if you're gay?'

'Gay?' he echoed again.

'Lord, is that the wrong term, too?' Dee was beginning to wish she'd talked about the weather instead. 'I thought homosexuals didn't mind being called that.'

He seemed to finally catch up with the conversation.'Who told you I was homosexual?'

'You did, earlier. Remember?'

'Vaguely.'

'Don't worry,' she assured him. 'I won't go advertising it.'

He seemed about to say something. Dee had the strong impression he was going to deny it. She hoped he wouldn't. She was beginning to like him, but she couldn't stand liars.

In the end, however, he said without much conviction, 'That's good to hear.'

'I won't, *honestly,*' Dee stressed. 'And it's not as if it's obvious. I mean you look very masculine, really.'

'Should I take that as a compliment?' he asked in ironic tones.

'No.'

'I thought not.'

Dee pulled a slight face and wished he would stop trying to put her on the spot.

They lapsed into silence as Rick came to set the table in front of them.

When he'd gone, the stranger asked, 'Where is this squat?'

'In a block of maisonettes the council have condemned.'

'How long have you lived there?'

'About six weeks.'

He frowned. 'And the council haven't noticed?'

'Why should they?' She shrugged. 'I've left it boarded up, and the electricity and gas are still disconnected. Even if they did know, they wouldn't care. They're pulling it down for redevelopment soon.'

'And then what? Where will you go?'

The questions could have denoted genuine interest, but Dee was doubtful. 'Why? Are you doing a documentary or something? "The plight of the homeless?" Been done before, mate, sorry.'

'No, I am not making a documentary.' He kept his patience—just. 'I was simply wondering if you'd made any contingency plans for the summer.'

'Well, I was hoping to go cruising the Greek islands again,' Dee replied in the same flippant tones, 'but my boat's in dry dock at the moment.'

His mouth tightened. 'Don't you take anything seriously?'

'Like life, you mean?' She slanted him a look wise beyond her years. 'And where do you think that would get me—taking the long-term view?'

Baxter saw her point. With nothing to look forward to and no way of lifting herself up out of her current situation, maybe it was best to take each day as it came.

'Have you no qualifications?' he asked in a manner that suggested he expected she had none.

Dee decided to surprise him with the truth. 'Nine GCSES—six As, two Bs and a D. I'm still working on my A levels.'

Baxter grimaced at what he took for sarcasm. 'Okay, message received. You want me to mind my own business.'

Actually, no. Dee had wanted him to be impressed. To look at her in a new light. To talk to her as if she were worth talking to. But, no, she was just another homeless no-hoper to him—and to almost every other person who passed her on their way to work and the real world.

'Give the man a coconut,' she finally responded, just as Rick approached the table.

'Coconut?' Rick repeated, not much one for sarcasm. 'I don't serve coconuts. You want coconuts, go to one of those West Indian market stalls.' He dumped two plates in front of them and waited for some acknowledgement.

'Thanks, Rick,' Dee said, with a commendably straight face.

'Yes, thanks, Rick,' Baxter echoed, in a voice also laced with amusement.

They waited until Rick was out of range before they laughed together.

It was a brief lapse, but laughter transformed her. From a belligerent, cropped-haired punk to a bright-eyed, spirited girl-woman. The change fascinated Baxter.

Then she switched to being a child, eating her meal with wordless, indiscriminate haste.

Dee had grown used to going all day with a virtually empty stomach, not allowing herself to think of her hunger. When presented with food, however, that was all she could think of. She didn't look up until she'd finished every last scrap.

It was only then that she was aware of his eyes on her, only then that she realised how greedy she must seem.

His own plate remained untouched.

'How old are you?' he asked, not for the first time.

'Eighteen.' Well, she would be soon.

'Good,' he nodded.

'Good?' she quizzed.

'I was worried you might be a runaway,' he added, assuming she wasn't.

She had been. She had first left home last summer. It had been easy. She'd had it planned for months. She'd had cash, squirrelled away from birthdays, Christmas and pocket money. It had seemed a fortune, but it had gone after a matter of weeks and she'd returned home rather than live on the streets. Three months ago she'd run away again. This time no one had come looking for her.

'This thing I want you to do will be complicated enough—' he resumed the conversation, '—without any irate parents appearing on my doorstep.'

'There'll be no irate parents.' Her mother was many things—pretty, silly, vain—but never strong enough to be irate. 'So, if you're thinking of murdering me, you can be fairly sure I'll go unmourned,' she added with black humour.

It drew no smile in return. Instead he said tersely, 'If you thought there was any chance of my being a psychopath, why the hell did you go with me?'

'Why do you think?' she retorted. She waved the two halves of the notes in front of his face, as he'd done to her earlier. 'Anyway, you don't look much like a homicidal maniac... So, assuming you're not, what are you?'

He hesitated, his eyes narrowing as if he was testing her discretion.

'You're not an actor, are you?' Dee speculated.

'An actor?' His tone dismissed the idea. 'What makes you think that?'

'Because you're so good-looking, I suppose,' she admitted quite frankly. Of course, she wouldn't have done so had he been straight. But he wasn't, so it didn't count.

He was taken aback for a moment, then said, 'Are you always so forthright with men?'

'No, not with—' Dee caught herself up, about to use the word 'normal'. It was a minefield, trying to be politically correct. She switched to saying, 'Not with some men. You know—macho types that interpret "hello" as an invitation to sleep with you.'

His brows rose before he commented, 'I suppose I should be grateful you don't class me in that category.'

'No, well, you couldn't be, could you?' Dee continued to display a newly discovered tactless streak. She dismissed a prospective career in the diplomatic service and ran on, 'Does that mean you're not an actor?'

'Sorry to disappoint you,' he drawled back, 'but I'm something a shade more pedestrian.'

She lifted a questioning brow.

'Pedestrian—that means—'

'Commonplace, ordinary, mundane… Yes, I know.'

'Sorry, I thought—'

'That "homeless" equated with "ignorant",' she cut in. 'Well, don't feel too bad. It's a fairly universal reaction.'

Baxter found he didn't feel bad so much as disconcerted. He was used to being in charge, the senior man in most situations. But he suspected this smart-mouthed girl would be no respecter of age or position.

He tried her out, saying, 'Actually, I'm a doctor.'

He waited for her reaction. Usually people were *over*-impressed by his profession.

Dee gave a brief, surprised laugh. It was some coincidence.

'Well, no one's ever found it amusing before,' he said with a slight edge to his voice.

She shrugged without apology. 'You don't look the part, though I suppose you're a big hit with the female patients.' Once more she forgot his sexual orientation.

'And why do you think that?' he enquired dryly.

Dee found herself colouring under his amused gaze before muttering, 'As I said earlier, you're very good-looking. I imagine you'd send a few hearts fluttering—whether you wanted to or not.'

'Hearts fluttering?' He raised a brow. 'Who would have thought a romantic lay under such a cynical exterior?'

Dee realised he was taking the mickey, and said coldly, 'I was being ironic. You know what I mean.'

'Not personally, no,' he denied. 'Most of my patients are too busy dying on me to notice my physical appearance.'

He spoke so dryly Dee wondered if he was joking, but something in his eyes told her he wasn't.

'I used to work for an aid agency in Africa,' he explained briefly.

It was Dee who pursued it. 'In famine areas, that kind of thing?'

He nodded, but, though her interest was patent, he didn't capitalise on it. Instead he turned to eating his meal.

Dee studied him surreptitiously across the table, wondering if it was true. She knew several doctors. Her father had been one—harassed and overworked, dedicated in the beginning, a burnt-out man in the end. Her stepfather was something else, a hospital consultant with expensive tastes and no real interest in medicine besides what it could earn him. Their doctor friends had been somewhere in between.

But this stranger was different. She couldn't categorise him.

'That must be challenging,' she finally replied, and immediately realised what an inadequate word it was to use for such work.

He probably thought so too, from the brief, tight smile on his mouth, but he let it pass.

Before she could make a fool of herself again, Dee asked, 'So what sort of job could you possibly want me to do, Doc?'

He pulled a face at the 'Doc'. 'I'll tell you in a minute. First I want you to understand something. If you decide you don't want a part of it, then I have to warn you. You shouldn't waste your time going to the police or the newspapers or anyone else, because I'll simply deny it all... And you know who people will believe?'

Not her, Dee acknowledged silently, and felt like kicking herself. It was illegal, this job of his. Of course it was. What had she expected?

She began to rise to her feet, and a hand shot out to keep her there. 'Where are you going?'

'Forget it.' She thrust the two halves of money at him. 'If it's illegal, I'm out of here.'

'It isn't,' Baxter lied without conscience, and felt relief as she subsided back in her chair. Then a thought occurred to him. 'You aren't already in trouble with the police, are you?'

'*No, I am not!*' she declared indignantly.

'Okay, okay,' he pacified her, although inwardly disputing her right to be outraged after the fare-dodging incident. 'I was just checking. I don't need any additional hassles…I assume you're single, too?'

'Single?'

'As in unmarried.'

'Of course.' Dee laughed, conveying how little she thought of marriage. '—Why?'

Baxter hesitated, then finally decided to get round to the reason he'd approached this waif and stray.

He grimaced before relaying the information. 'You can't be married because that's part of the job—getting married.'

Getting married? Dee repeated the words to herself, as if by doing so they might take on a new meaning, but they didn't. Then she took to staring at him as if he were completely and utterly mad.

He wanted her to marry him and she didn't even know his name!

CHAPTER TWO

'I DON'T even know your name,' Dee said aloud.

'Baxter,' he introduced himself, as if that would make it less ridiculous.

'Look, Mr Baxter...' She intended to tell him what he could do with his job.

'It's not Mr Baxter,' he corrected, 'it's—'

'I know,' Dee cut across him. 'Mustn't forget the title, must we? *Dr* Baxter.'

Her tone was derisive. He was not perturbed.

'Actually, I was about to say it's Ross.'

'Ross?

'*Mr* Ross, if we're going in for formalities.' A slanting smile mocked her in return. 'I'm not hung up on the "Dr" bit.'

Having made a fool of herself, Dee didn't exactly feel more warmly disposed towards him. 'Baxter. That's your first name?' she concluded, and, at his nod, muttered, 'What kind of name is that?'

'A Scottish one.'

'Well, that explains it.'

Baxter knew he shouldn't ask. But he did. 'Explains what?'

'Why you talk funny,' Dee replied with careless rudeness.

'*I* talk funny?' He laughed at the sheer nerve of the girl. 'Well, at least my accent doesn't go walkabout.'

'What do you mean?' She glared back.

But Baxter reckoned she knew well enough. 'What I can't quite figure,' he ran on, 'is which one's real—the cockney sparrow routine or the middle-class girl from the Home Counties?'

'You don't need to figure it—' his perception disconcerted Dee '—because neither is crazy enough to marry you!'

He listened without expression, any insult lost on him. Mr Cool.

'I didn't actually ask you to marry me,' he said at length.

Dee scowled. Perhaps he hadn't said the words, but that was surely his intent. He was just splitting hairs now.

'So what else were you doing? Asking me to marry someone else?' Her tone told him that would rate as even crazier.

He hesitated fractionally before saying, 'Whichever, it's an irrelevancy. It would, naturally, be what's termed a marriage of convenience.'

'No sex, you mean.' Dee had no time for silly euphemisms. 'I'd kinda worked that out for myself... You need me as camouflage, right?'

'Camouflage?'

'You want to convince the world you're straight, and you reckon what better way than to acquire a wife. Only you don't want a real wife, because then she'd expect you to...well, you get my drift.'

'I think so.' Baxter realised she was on a completely different road, but possibly they'd arrive at the same destination in time. So why throw her off-course for now?

Dee watched the thoughts crossing his handsome face and imagined she could read them. She relented slightly, saying, 'Look, I really have no problem with your being gay, and if you want to keep it a secret I can understand that too. But maybe life would be easier if you simply ''outed'' yourself. Just made a one-off declaration to the world, then just got on with your life...

Lots of people do it—TV personalities, actors, pop stars. You could almost call it fashionable... And you know what they say about honesty being the best policy and all that.'

'I doubt it applies in this case.' Baxter realised her sudden sympathy only applied because she thought he was gay.

'Well, it's your life.' Dee decided she wasn't in the best shape to be advising anyone else. 'And I suppose a marriage of convenience rates one better than pretending to do it for real.'

'Sorry?' She'd lost him again.

'It's what some gay men do,' she ran on. 'Marry, have kids even, then, hey presto, they hit mid-life crisis and leave their wives for another man.'

'You're an authority on this, are you?' he enquired dryly.

'Not especially,' she denied. 'I just had a schoolfriend whose father did it... They were all devastated,' she recalled matter-of-factly.

'Do you know anyone with happy, uncomplicated lives?' he asked when she'd finished this gloomy tale.

'No—do you?' she flipped back.

Her tone said she didn't believe in happiness. Baxter wondered what had made her so cynical.

'Actually, yes,' he responded. 'My sister, Catriona, and her husband have a marriage that seems reasonably close to perfect.'

'*Seems* being the operative word,' Dee couldn't resist commenting. From her own experience she knew so-called perfect marriages could hide cracks the size of the San Andreas fault line. Take her mother and stepfather. The world had always seen them as the perfect couple. Come to that, the world probably still did—the perfect couple cursed only by a bad lot of a daughter.

Dee had no illusions. It was what people had thought of her. A bad lot that would come to a worse end.

'Well, you'll be able to judge for yourself.' His voice broke into her thoughts once more.

'Judge what?'

'If it's real, their happiness... But I'm warning you now. They do a great deal of laughing and smiling, and even kissing. So it may be hard for a world-weary cynic like yourself to take.'

He was laughing, too. At her, in this case. Dee tried to take offence, but there was something disarming about the smile he slanted her.

'I haven't agreed to anything,' she said instead, then realised it wasn't quite positive enough. 'I mean, I can't possibly do what you're suggesting.'

'Why not?'

Why not? Dee repeated to herself, and didn't immediately find an answer. A smile touched his lips as he detected her weakening.

She shook her head. 'You expect me to go up to the wilds of Scotland—'

'We live about fifteen miles from the centre of Edinburgh,' he interjected. 'Almost civilisation, in fact.'

'Okay, but then there's the time.' She raised a new objection. 'Or are you planning for me to go up on one train, play blushing bride for a day, then take the next train home? I doubt that'll convince anyone.'

'No, you'd obviously have to commit to longer. Let's say a year's contract.'

'*A year!*'

'At the very most.' He nodded. 'But if things go well I'd release you earlier.'

'Release me?' she echoed. 'This is beginning to sound like a prison sentence.'

'Not quite. You won't be on bread and water, or sewing mailbags,' he assured her in dry tones. 'Basically, you'll have your own room, three square meals a day and a moderate allowance. Will that be so bad?'

'Sounds wonderful,' she said, but gave a visible shudder as she ran on. 'Going quietly out of my head, playing the little woman at home.'

Baxter laughed in response. Not very wise at this stage of the negotiation, but it was just too absurd.

'*You?* The little woman? Apart from looking totally unlike the part, I somehow doubt you'd be that good an actress.'

'Thanks.' She pulled a face. 'So why ask me?'

Good question, Baxter had to agree. 'There wasn't exactly a wide choice of candidates.'

'And beggars can't be choosers?' Dee threw his earlier words back at him.

'Something like that.' He didn't deny it.

'You're crazy,' Dee said aloud, then silently to herself. For she had to be crazy, too, listening to this.

He said nothing, but took out a pen and chequebook from the inside pocket of his jacket. Dee watched as he wrote in it, then stared in disbelief as he held the cheque in front of her face.

'That's what you'll get on the day of the wedding,' he relayed to her, 'and then the same at the end of twelve months, or whenever I release you.'

Five thousand pounds. Double that by the end. She read and reread it, wondering if she was hallucinating and seeing too many noughts.

'You're kidding!' she scoffed.

'Scotsmen don't kid about money.' He placed the cheque on the table before her. 'Don't you know that?'

He smiled, as if it might still turn out to be a joke, but his eyes said different. This was business.

It was Dee who shook her head. This was fantasy. 'You'll pay me ten thousand pounds just to marry you?'

'You think that's too much?' he returned.

Dee's lips formed the word 'Yes' but she didn't utter it aloud. Did she really want to talk the price down?

'Make no mistake. It's up to a year of your life—and that's a long time at your age,' he warned, eyes resting on her as if assessing just how young she was.

'How old are *you?*' Dee threw back at him.

'Thirty-four.' He watched her screw up her face and added, 'Virtually geriatric to you, I imagine.'

That wasn't actually what Dee had been thinking, 'Have you considered what other people are going to make of the age gap? I mean there's not much point in hiring me for a respectable front if my appearance is going to result in the opposite.'

'For ten thousand pounds, I expect you could modify your appearance,' he suggested, without going into details.

He didn't have to. His gaze went from her earrings in triplicate to her close-cropped haircut.

Dee knew how she looked, with her hair and her combat jacket and her laced up Doc Martens—like a tough neo-punk who could take care of herself. It was exactly how she wanted to look. When her hair had been longer and her clothes more feminine, she'd had to fend off the pimps and perverts who preyed on girls in her situation.

'I expect I could,' Dee echoed, 'if I was mad enough to

go along with you. But let's get real. You think anybody—
your family or friends—is going to believe we're each other's types?'

Not in a million years, Baxter had to agree. His sister
might have spent the last decade trying to marry him off,
but even she would balk at this girl. Colleagues would
imagine he was having a mid-life crisis. And male friends,
unable to see any other virtue, would assume she was great
in bed. Still, none of that really mattered.

'Attraction of opposites?' he suggested, with a smile of
pure irony. 'Don't worry about it. It won't be a problem...
Just try and tone down a little before you come north of
the border. I can give you an advance for clothes if necessary.'

'Tweed skirts and twinsets?' she commented dryly, but
did wonder what image she was meant to cultivate.

'Up to you.' He shrugged, as if it was a small issue.

And Dee, realising he was being serious about the rest,
finally found herself considering it. What did she have to
lose?

'Well, how about it?' He was hardly pressurising her into
it.

'I don't know.' She was clearly wavering.

'Look, if you're concerned about being able to marry
someone else in the future,' he added, 'then don't be. I'll
finance the divorce, too.'

'That isn't an issue. I won't be getting married. Not for
real, anyway,' she amended.

'Ever?' He raised a brow.

'Ever,' she echoed with utter conviction.

'Don't tell me—you're off men for life.' He clearly
didn't take her seriously.

'Not all men—and just marriage.'

'A woman who doesn't automatically hear wedding
bells. Where have you been all my life?'

He was joking. She realised that. But still it seemed an
odd thing for him to say.

She stared at him hard. 'I didn't think you were interested in women.'

Baxter stared back briefly, before deciding to come clean.

'Time to set the record straight, I think—straight being the appropriate word.'

Dee took a moment to catch on. 'You're not gay?'

''Fraid not,' he confided in ironic tones.

Something about his manner made Dee believe him. She should have been angry—and she was—but, behind that, she also felt an odd sense of relief.

She didn't let it show as she demanded, 'So why did you say you were?'

'Technically I didn't,' he corrected. 'What I said was, "I'm not interested in young girls". Which I'm not, preferring a more mature kind of woman... So, you're still safe.'

Safe, but confused. 'Then why the arranged marriage?'

'That's harder to explain.' He was obviously in no hurry to do so.

Dee, impatient as ever, jumped to another conclusion. 'I bet it's a legacy. You have to get married by your thirty-fifth birthday or you'll be disinherited by some great-aunt. Am I right?'

Baxter raised a mental eyebrow. She certainly had imagination. He just wasn't sure yet if he could trust her with the truth.

'It's connected with a legacy, yes,' he finally confirmed.

'I knew it!' She looked pleased with herself for guessing.

'Anyway, I can't go into details at the moment,' he asserted. 'I can only stress once more that it will *just* be a marriage of convenience.'

He didn't have to stress it. Dee had got the message. He didn't fancy her. Did he have to keep labouring the point?

'Well?' he added, raising a brow.

Decision time. 'I'd have to take Henry.'

'Of course.' He glanced down at the dog stretched at their feet. 'He seems a fairly well-behaved animal. Does he like trains?'

'Is that how we'd be travelling...assuming I agreed?'

He nodded. 'I haven't been back long from Kirundi, and am currently carless.'

'You were in Kirundi?' Dee read newspapers and magazines dumped in the underground by commuters. She knew something of the civil war that had raged in the African country.

He nodded. 'For the last couple of years.'

He sounded emotionless about it, but how could he be? It must have been a scene from hell.

'Are you going back?' she asked.

He shook his head. 'I have no plans to do so.'

Dee met his eyes briefly and imagined she saw in them some of the shadows of that hell. It was just a fleeting impression before he looked away, but she knew without being told; she mustn't ask any more.

'My contract with the aid agency has just run out,' he continued. 'I'll be taking up a research post at Edinburgh University in the autumn.'

Dee absorbed this information, then said, 'Okay, give me the time of the train and we can meet at the station.'

It was a moment before he realised quite what she'd said.

'You'll do it?' Her capitulation had caught him by surprise.

Dee wondered if she really was mad, even as she nodded, 'Yeah, why not?'

'Great.' Baxter suppressed any doubts and allowed himself some satisfaction.

Dee decided it was time to go before she changed her mind. 'If you don't know times and things, you can phone Rick in the café. He'll pass on a message.'

He glanced towards Rick, who was now leaning on the counter, perusing the racing pages. He didn't look the reliable type.

'Wouldn't it make more sense for me to pick you up in a taxi?' he suggested.

'You mean turn up at the squat?' She was horrified by the idea. 'No, thanks. I'll meet you at the station or the deal's off.'

Baxter realised she didn't want him to know where she lived. He supposed that was fair enough from her angle.

He went into his pocket again and found his passport, still there from when he'd flown in a few days ago. He handed it to her.

Dee checked it over, as he'd intended. It came open at

the back pages; they were stamped with the names of a dozen countries, mostly in Africa. She flipped to the front and glanced at his picture. It was an old passport, showing a picture of him from some years ago. It looked like him, only without the current signs of age and experience. She checked the other details. Name: Baxter Macfarlane Ross. Occupation: Doctor. Birthplace: Bangkok.

'Bangkok.' She read it aloud. 'As in Bangkok, Thailand?'

'My parents were missionaries,' he explained. 'They happened to be trying to convert South-East Asia round the time of my birth.'

'So where exactly were you brought up?'

'Lots of places, but Scotland mainly. That's where our grandparents lived and that's where we were sent to school.'

'Boarding school?' she guessed, and he nodded in response.

It explained a lot. He had no real accent, despite the fact she'd made a joke of it earlier. Instead he sounded neutral, almost as if he was a foreigner who'd learned to speak perfect English.

'So, do your parents live up in Edinburgh?' she asked, and felt a measure of relief when he shook his head. She didn't fancy playing the blushing bride to some holy rollers who probably still believed in marriage.

'They died when I was twelve,' he added briefly.

'Sorry,' Dee apologised for her mean thoughts.

'It was a long time ago.' He dismissed any need for sensitivity. 'And I didn't know them well... My sister lives near me.'

'Oh.' So she was to meet some of his family. 'Are you and your sister close?'

'Yes and no. I've spent a large part of my adult life abroad... What about you? Do you have any brothers or sisters?'

'No, I'm a little emperor.' She'd read the expression in a magazine.

'A what?'

'An only child. It's what they call them in China, now they operate a one-child policy... Apparently couples in

Britain are also opting to have a single child so they can give them everything.'

'Is that what you were given...everything?' He wondered once more about this girl of contradictions.

'Of course,' she answered in ironic tones. 'As you see, I dine at the Ritz, buy my clothes from Harvey Nichols and live in a darling little mews house in South Kensington.'

He gave her an impatient look. 'I take it that means no.'

Dee shrugged. He could take it how he wanted. In truth she had been spoilt—materially anyway—until the day she had run away in her state-of-the-art trainers, designer jeans, and the baseball jacket that had come with a three-hundred-pound price tag and had fallen apart within weeks of her hitting the London streets.

She handed back his passport, and he said, 'Now you know who I am, perhaps you could trust me with your address.'

'Just because you're *Dr* Ross?' She pulled a face, still unimpressed.

'Point taken.' He took one of the cheap paper napkins Rick had tossed down in front of them and wrote something on it.

'The Continental,' Dee read. 'Sounds posh.'

He ignored her, writing down the nearest tube station and precise directions on how to find the hotel. 'Meet me in the foyer tomorrow at nine o'clock, and we'll go shopping for suitable clothing. Okay?'

Dee nodded and put the napkin in her jacket. She didn't meet his eyes. If she had, he might have realised she was already having second thoughts. Girls who met up with strangers, however respectable-looking, were asking for trouble.

Baxter watched her as she got up, issued brief thanks for the meal, and, gathering her possessions and dog, made for the door. He was no fool. Chances were he would never see her again.

Dee walked quickly, checking behind her a few times, but there was no sign of him. He trusted her. He actually believed she was going to meet him.

'Mug,' she muttered aloud, but it didn't stop her feeling

guilty. She hadn't meant to lead him on. It was his fault really. It had sounded so attractive—sleeping in a clean bed, eating good food, earning money for virtually nothing.

But nothing was for nothing in this life. She knew better. She thought of her stepfather—respected consultant, charming host, generous father. For a while, at least, until he'd looked for the pay-back.

Dee put a brake on her thoughts. She wasn't going to get bitter. She wouldn't let him ruin her life. She wasn't like the other girls, running away from a lifetime of abuse. Much of her childhood had been happy, and she still had hopes of a future better than her dismal present.

She checked behind her once more before she veered towards the wasteland which surrounded the maisonettes. All boarded up, they looked deserted, but she knew that several had been turned into squats. Hers was at the end of the block and two flights up.

She looked along the balcony and down below, checking she was alone, before dislodging the loose boarding at the bottom of a window. Then she squeezed through and dragged Henry after her. She replaced the boarding and used a brick to hold it in position from the inside. She kept a torch in her rucksack, and used it long enough to locate the candles and matches hidden under the rotting sink-cupboard.

She slept in a back room, where the last occupant had abandoned an old mattress. It was stained and musty, but better than the floor. Dee had her own sleeping bag, which she washed with her clothes at the launderette when she had any spare money. She still never felt clean.

She'd lived like this, in one squat or another, for three months, and she'd begun to get used to it. She supposed it was meeting Baxter Ross that had made her re-evaluate. She went to the toilet and looked in the cracked mirror above the sink. A gaunt face with hollow eyes looked back at her. Once she'd been considered pretty, and was vain enough to wonder if anyone would see her as such again. Or had her looks gone, along with her middle-class attitudes? Blown away by insecurity and desperation?

She thought of what Baxter Ross was offering. Right at

the moment it was the only chance of a future she had. Perhaps she was crazy to turn it down. It would mean living a lie, but so what? She had watched her mother doing that for years.

Had her mother pretended with her father, too? Dee wasn't sure. She had seemed devastated when he died, but within months had been going out with Edward Litton, a consultant at the hospital.

At first Dee had resented it, out of loyalty to her father. But, as time went on, she'd realised her mother couldn't cope on her own. Edward had seemed to accept her so she'd accepted Edward, and had been a gawky-looking bridesmaid at their wedding.

When had things changed? It was hard to pinpoint, but it seemed, on reflection, that cracks had appeared in the marriage quite quickly. Though beautiful, her mother needed constant reassurance of the fact, and although seemingly vivacious in company, was subject to depressions. Dee's father had been supportive, but Edward was a different kind of man, and his impatience, as well as his disappointment, was evident.

At times Dee had actually felt sorry for him and had feared he might leave. Feared, because at fourteen she had been as selfish as the next teenager and hadn't wanted responsibility for her mother's happiness.

But they'd papered over the cracks and continued to present an idyllic front to the rest of the world. Dee had been part of the conspiracy, then. Grateful that he'd stayed, she'd grown closer to Edward, and he had seemed fond of her, too.

It was Edward who had begun to realise she was growing up and had given her money for trendy clothes rather than the juvenile outfits her mother had bought to keep her looking about ten—which had been difficult when she was already way past adult height by fourteen and filling out by fifteen. It was Edward who had allowed her to go to her first disco and had laughed when she'd arrived home a little tipsy. Edward who hadn't overreacted to her minor teenage rebellions of smoking cigarettes and bunking off school. And Edward who'd argued against boarding school, claiming that, just going into her final GCSE year at sixteen, Deborah was far too old to adapt.

Only this time her mother had stood her ground, and Dee had been dispatched to a girls' school in Hampshire. Dee had minded going, but had settled in surprisingly easily. After the tensions at home, the school regime had been almost relaxing.

Still, she'd looked forward to the Christmas holidays, and Edward and her mother had both seemed pleased to see her. There had been the usual seasonal parties, and Edward had paid for several new dresses—including a white mini-dress that showed off her endless legs. She had been self-conscious in it at first, but had worn it at their New Year party and felt tremendously grown-up.

Perhaps she had looked it, too, because no one had objected to her drinking glasses of the wine being passed around. She had been merry rather than drunk, and had danced a lot with an older boy called James. They had ended up kissing in the summerhouse outside. Deborah had enjoyed the kisses and even allowed some minor petting, but she'd had no plans to take things further.

Edward had drawn other conclusions when he'd found them in a passionate clinch. He'd come the heavy father and sent the boy packing, then he'd turned on Dee. She remembered repeating, 'Nothing happened,' over and over, but he hadn't really been listening as he'd grabbed her arm when she'd tried to leave. It was only later she had understood: he'd been drunk, and mean with it.

At the time she'd felt only shame as he'd accused her of being a slut and suggested she'd been 'begging for it'. There had been more of the same, but, naively, she hadn't been frightened. Even at that point she'd still assumed he was acting like an irate grown-up. Then the bile about her mother had begun to spill out, and effectively brought their father-daughter relationship to an end.

'Please.' She tried to pull away as he regaled her with details of his empty, sexless marriage.

'Well, at least we know *you're* not frigid, little Deborah,' he went on relentlessly. 'Not so little, either, now…'

His eyes lowered to her burgeoning breasts, outlined in

the brief, tight dress, and the hand that had gripped her arm began to smooth over her bare skin.

Dee fought panic and the desire to be physically sick. This was a nightmare. In a moment, they would both wake up and everything would be as before.

'Let's go back to the party, Edward, please...' Her face was white with shock.

'Why? So you can let that boy paw you again?' Edward's laugh was humourless as he blocked her move to the summerhouse door. 'Sweet sixteen and obviously dying for it, the way you walk around the house in your shortie nightdresses.'

Dee shook her head and kept shaking it, denying provocation, denying she wanted this, denying his right to do it as he clamped his arms round her and forced his mouth on hers, ignoring her resistance, his teeth cutting into her lip, his tongue a violation. She resisted, and kept resisting, twisting and fighting, kicking and squirming, pushing at his chest until finally, somehow, she was free.

She turned and ran blindly to the house. The party was still in full swing and few noticed as she burst inside and made for the toilet, bolting the door before being violently sick in the bowl.

Dee had intended to tell her mother later, but Edward beat her to it. In his version she had drunk too much and had been throwing herself at everybody, including himself. He made a joke of it, then dismissed the incident as normal adolescence. Her mother didn't question it, and when Dee tried to say Edward had kissed her she refused to listen.

Now Dee lay on her mattress in the dirty squat and recognised it as the night her childhood had ended. She hadn't run away immediately; she hadn't been brave enough. She'd wanted to trust Edward's promises that it would never happen again, so she had. Until the next time two months later. And the time after that at half term. And so on.

Each time he went a little further and each time she became more locked in the awful conspiracy of silence because she hadn't blown the whistle loudly enough that first night.

Each episode of kissing or touching or accidentally brushing against her brought them closer to the day he would finally rape her. She threatened to tell on him, but never did. Who to tell? Her mother, who popped a pill at the least upset and was on another planet most of the time? Or family friends, who admired Edward for taking on a ready-made family? And, of course, by not telling she re-inforced the lies her stepfather was telling himself: that *she* wanted *him* the same way he wanted her.

When he arrived mid-term to take her out for a surprise lunch, Dee wanted to refuse, but what could she say when he sat in the headmistress's office playing model stepfather? And who else could see what lay behind his smile? Not Mrs Chambers, smiling back as good old Edward charmed and smarmed his way into her confidence. Not her best friend, Clare, who read too many teen magazines and thought her stepfather sexy.

So she went upstairs for her jacket and came down the hard way, throwing herself from the landing. Dramatic, possibly, and certainly painful, as the sprained ankle she'd intended escalated into a torn ligament in her knee. She also had to suffer Edward playing the concerned father and caring doctor, until she wanted to scream at them all, *Open your eyes. See him for what he is!*

But still it was worth it. A trip to the local hospital took precedence over the lunch.

It was that visit which decided her. She waited until her knee mended and the exams were over, then bought a one-way ticket to London. She stayed in a cheap hotel, unable to find work or the bedsit she'd vaguely planned. After a month and a half her money ran out, and she ended up sleeping in a shop doorway for three nights until the police picked her up, and, not believing she was sixteen, located her on a register of runaways and called her parents.

They came to collect her. Her mother was distressed but forgiving, while Edward just seemed relieved. He walked up to her and hugged her as he had in the old days, with a warmth that was natural and fatherly, and promised her everything was going to be fine. After three nights' sleeping rough and being terrified, Dee would have believed the devil himself. She arrived home in time for her seventeenth birthday and was lavished with presents.

For eight months Edward kept his promise. Dee didn't give him much choice to do otherwise, returning to boarding school in the autumn, then spending much of the Christmas holidays on a skiing trip. Then she made the mistake of going home for Easter.

At seventeen, and confident, she imagined she could handle anything, but she was wrong.

She had no real warning. That was the trouble. Her mother had a headache, but that wasn't unusual. Dee sat down to lunch with Edward and he was in great form, relating amusing anecdotes about hospital life. She didn't really notice him filling and refilling his glass. She wasn't aware of a mood change until it was too late...

Dee shut her eyes now. She didn't want to relive it. What had happened had seemed unreal, but was no less disturbing because of it. She had panicked and she had run, and this time no one had come looking for her.

She had no home now, no family, no past. She could do what she wanted, be what she wanted. She could marry Baxter Ross for ten thousand pounds and not give a damn.

Why not? Would it be so hard to be Mrs Baxter Ross?

She wouldn't have to sleep with him. She probably wouldn't have to eat with him either. Talking might not even be required, unless they had an audience.

Ten thousand pounds, and she could lie in a clean bed without listening for every sound in the dark, eat without worrying about where the next meal was coming from, live without fear constantly in the background.

In fact, even a cynic like Dee could see it—Baxter Ross just had to be a dream come true!

CHAPTER THREE

WHAT was the opposite of a guardian angel? A jinx, Dee supposed. Whatever it was, she had one.

Having tossed and turned for most of the night, she slept when the first rays of light squeezed through the boarded windows and only woke when the air was warm and the sun high in the sky. She didn't need a watch to tell her she was already far too late. She would never reach the Continental Hotel by nine.

She went all the same, with Henry in tow, and used her last money on the fare. The hotel was posh and exclusive, and its doorman wouldn't let her past the steps. Reluctant enquiries were made. They confirmed a Dr Ross had been there—*had* being the operative word. It was her fault for being late, but she cursed him all the same. Couldn't he just have waited?

She drifted off to the nearest tube station and, without a flute to play, did what she hated and begged outright. Her dismal face drew little sympathy, but enough for her fare home, tea and a roll at Rick's and two tins of dog food.

She made her way home, thinking the day couldn't get worse, but it did. She saw the caravans first, parked at the near end of the estate. For a moment she thought they belonged to gypsies, until she saw the vans on the other side and was whistled at by two workmen swilling beers on a caravan step. The developers were moving in.

She raced along to her maisonette, thinking she might already be too late to fetch her stuff, but the flats still stood, doors and windows now plastered with orders to quit and a demolition date two days hence.

She'd known it would be soon. When she'd found the place there had been other squatters around her, but most had since disappeared. She rounded the corner of her block to find the couple from downstairs passing stuff out through a gap in their boarding.

They claimed to have somewhere to go and invited Dee to come along with them, but Dee felt safer on her own.

She went up to her flat and was relieved to find the boarding still in place. She helped Henry in first, because he was too stiff to manage on his own. She collected her things together, ready to move on in the morning, then sat on her dirty mattress, trying not to think of the chance she'd let slip by.

It was some hours later when she heard noises again. They were distant at first, probably coming from the far end of the block. She heard the sound of splintering wood. A board being moved. Perhaps it was someone like herself, looking for a place to sleep. Usually she laid low, waiting for whoever it was to settle.

This time, however, it seemed they were checking every flat, searching for something or somebody, and Dee no longer felt like sitting tight. So she slipped through the gap in the boarding and landed soundlessly on the balcony below, then tried to haul Henry through, but he kept backing away. Having been reluctant to wake, he was even more reluctant to go walking.

Dee heard footsteps directly below her and, panic rising, made another grab for his collar. Unfortunately Henry began to whine and scrape and generally protest at the idea of going through the narrow gap for the second time that day. She leaned further and Henry disappeared altogether in the direction of the bedroom.

Dee might have climbed back in, but the footsteps were no longer below her; they were echoing up the far stairwell. As she withdrew from the window her jacket caught on a nail. The sleeve ripped slightly, then held fast. Rather than rip it further, she shrugged out of it and left it hanging as, in panic, she took to her heels along the balcony towards the other staircase.

A voice called out, meaning to halt her, but all it did was make Dee's heart hammer with more fright. This was no kid out to vandalise a derelict building, but a full-grown man, and he was after her, his footsteps thundering in pur-

suit as she jumped three steps onto the landing, then stumbled her way down the next flight.

She landed hard and felt a jarring in her knee, but she
kept going. She made for the open wasteland and the cover
of darkness. But he was right behind her, running hard,
gaining on her, closing in as her knee began to give out.
She kept running until the second he grabbed at her, then
she cried out in fear and rage as she went crashing to the
ground.

Hard male hands kept her there. Face down in weeds and
muck, she waited for her worst nightmare to begin. Seconds
ticked by in her head before her assailant dragged her
round, and it was the longest moment in Dee's life.
Nothing, not even her experiences with her stepfather, had
prepared her for this.

Then he spoke, and fear dissolved in an instant. Relief
followed, but was quickly sidelined by temper.

She lifted a hand and struck at him.

'It's me…Baxter.' He warded off the blow.

'I know it's damn well you!' she screamed back at him,
and took another swipe.

He dodged that one, then grabbed at her arms before she
could hit him again. 'I'm not going to harm you.'

'No, just break my leg in a rugby tackle!' she shot back.

'I *was* trying to grab your arm,' he claimed, 'but you
halted mid-flight and I fell with you… Sorry.'

'*Sorry!*' Dee exploded at this utterly inadequate word.

He lifted his shoulders. 'What else can I say?'

'Try goodbye,' snapped a still angry Dee, 'but first could
you bloody well get off me?'

He considered it for a moment. 'Provided you promise
not to attack me again.'

Her attack *him?* Dee stared at him in disbelief.
Unfortunately, being flat on her back, she was in no position to argue.

'Okay,' she agreed.

'Good.'

'Come on then.'

Dee wasn't scared of him any longer. There was something so calm and rational about this man, it was hard to

imagine him as a threat. But she was still lying beneath him, conscious of the weight of his body on hers.

'I'm waiting,' he drawled.

'What for?'

'Your promise.'

God, he wanted her to dot the 'i's and cross the 't's.

'I promise not to attack you,' Dee ground out through clenched teeth.

Baxter caught her eyes, a stormy blue spitting fury. He released her arms slowly and half expected another blow. But perhaps she wasn't quite that foolish. She remained still as death beneath him, and he levered himself away. He brushed earth and undergrowth from his clothes before offering her a hand.

Dee ignored it. She knew she'd damaged her knee and wasn't sure if she could stand.

She shot at him instead, 'What are you doing here, anyway?'

'Looking for you,' he responded evenly. 'I assume you've backed out on our deal?'

Dee could have contradicted him, but right at that moment she couldn't see herself tolerating five minutes of his company, far less a year.

'How did you know where I was?'

'Your friend from the café gave me the general location.'

'Rick's no one's friend. How much did you give him in return?'

'Twenty pounds.'

'You were robbed,' she scoffed. 'Rick would sell his own mother for a fiver.'

He shook his head at her cynicism. 'You underrate his loyalty. It took me a while to convince him I meant you no harm.'

'I know—you told him of our engagement!' Dee concluded archly.

'Not quite.' His brief smile acknowledged the absurdity of such a relationship. 'I said you were my runaway niece.'

'How original—the niece story again,' she scorned. 'I hope you didn't tell him my real name was Morag!'

'I had to. I don't know your real name.' He lifted a questioning brow.

'Deborah DeCourcy,' she told him.

He laughed in disbelief. 'Okay, don't tell me, but I'd aim for something more credible next time.'

'That is my name,' she insisted. 'And you should talk, *Mr Baxter Macfarlane Ross.*'

'I suppose it is a mouthful... All right, Deborah,' he tried out her new name.

She snapped, 'Don't call me that.'

'I thought it was your name,' he countered.

'It is. I just don't like it.' Deborah belonged to the girl Dee used to be. She was someone else now. 'You haven't answered my question. Why did you come looking for me?'

'To give you these.' He went into his jacket for his wallet and took out the other halves of the notes from yesterday. 'I thought you might need it.'

Dee took them and muttered a grudging, 'Thanks.'

'I wanted to check you were all right, too,' he added.

'Never better.' Dee grimaced as she struggled to her feet, and started limping back towards the flats.

'I can see that.' He caught her elbow and would have given her support, but she shrugged off his hand.

She made it as far as an abandoned oil drum, then perched on it for a rest.

He nodded towards her leg. 'Want me to take a look at that?'

'Why? What can you do?' Dee didn't want his concern.

'I'm a doctor, remember?'

Actually she hadn't. She still thought of him as male model material. Too handsome for words.

'So you say.' Dee had her doubts and didn't want him treating her anyway. 'You just don't happen to be *my* doctor.'

'No problem. I've got a mobile on me. Do you think *your* doctor will come on a house call?' He glanced round him at the derelict flats and urban wasteland.

'Very funny.' Dee understood the point. She didn't have a GP anyway.

'If you can't walk, I'll carry you,' he offered matter-of-factly.

'I'd rather die,' Dee muttered, not quite under her breath.

'Fair enough.' He began to walk away.

Dee watched in disbelief. 'You're not going to leave me here, are you?'

He turned, hands in pockets, and gave her a mocking look. 'What happened to "I'd rather die"!'

Dee could have thrown something at him, only she had nothing at hand. She made it to her feet instead, and hobbled a step or two.

He grunted his impatience before he came striding back and literally swept Dee off her feet. It was so unexpected, her heart missed a beat. Then missed another as she was compelled to lock her arms round his neck. Her hands brushed against the warmth of his skin while he moved with an easy strength. Unfamiliar feelings stirred inside her, and she tried to detach herself from this acute physical awareness of him.

'Stop squirming,' he instructed briskly as he picked his way past the debris of dumped rubbish and made for the road rather than her maisonette.

'Where are we going?' demanded Dee, alerted by the change of direction.

'There's a derelict bus shelter,' he informed her. 'You can sit there while I fetch the car.'

Car? What car? He'd said his car was in Scotland.

Could it all be a lie? His being a doctor, needing a wife, being willing to pay ten thousand pounds? The more Dee thought about it, the crazier it seemed.

He could be a liar, a thief, a madman, but the curious thing was, she still wasn't scared of him. In fact, as he dumped her in the graffitied bus shelter and wordlessly walked away, she was more scared that he wouldn't return.

By the time a car appeared and caught her in its headlights, she was very jumpy.

She was relieved when Baxter Ross emerged from behind the driver's wheel. He might be a stranger but there was something reassuringly normal about him.

He put an arm to her waist and helped her limp to the

car. She leaned on the bonnet and observed a car-hire sticker on the windscreen. So maybe he wasn't a liar.

He opened the passenger door, saying, 'I'll drive you to the nearest Casualty to check the damage.'

Dee already knew what was wrong; she had damaged the tendon again. 'I'll go tomorrow.'

He made a noise, impatient rather than sympathetic. 'Don't be silly. You won't get there under your own steam.'

'I have to go back to the maisonette,' she insisted.

He followed her worried glance to the block of flats. 'If it's a boyfriend, then he can't be up to much,' he dismissed. 'Not if he lets you go on midnight rambles in this neighbourhood.'

'It's a dog!' she retorted abruptly. 'You've met him, remember?'

'Yes, of course, Henry.' He surprised her by recalling her dog's name.

'I can't leave him,' she explained in more even tones. 'He'll be frightened on his own.'

'Get in.' He nodded towards the passenger seat. 'I'll go fetch the mutt.'

He was so offhand, it was impossible to imagine him as a threat. He started to walk away.

She called after him, 'Be careful. Henry might be a bit nervy.'

'Nervy—right.' He cast her a look over his shoulder. 'As in likely to bite first and ask questions later?'

'Possibly,' Dee admitted.

'Well, thanks for the warning, at least.' He carried on walking.

Dee watched him go, a tall, lean figure with a fluid stride. Nothing seemed to throw him.

It was Dee who felt reaction set in, shivering in the cool night air at her lack of jacket, and she climbed into the passenger seat to wait for him.

She soon heard barking, and rolled down the window a fraction. She worried about the dog initially, but as the barking became louder and fiercer her concern switched to

Baxter Ross. She might not like him much, but he was trying to help her when he could easily have walked away.

The barking continued, interspersed with the sound of wood being smashed, then there was silence. Dee sat in the car, holding her breath interminably, before they suddenly appeared.

The dog padded alongside the man. It seemed that Henry had decided Baxter Ross was more friend than foe. He wagged his tail, glad to see Dee but not unduly worried.

Dee watched in the mirror as Baxter Ross removed the parcel shelf at the back of the car and folded down the rear seats to create a large boot, pushing his own luggage nearer the front. He helped a stiff Henry into it and also stowed away her flute case and rucksack. Why had he brought those?

'Do you still want me to go to Scotland with you?' Dee asked as he climbed behind the wheel.

He turned and studied her face long enough to read the mutinous look on it. 'No, I think we'll abandon plan A. Some things are more trouble than they're worth.'

'Thanks.' Dee knew he meant *she* was more trouble than she was worth. 'So why are you bothering to help me?'

'I could say out of common decency, but I don't think you'd relate to that,' he responded, before starting the car and pulling away from the kerb. 'Let's say instead that I don't fancy being chief suspect if some psychopath happens to come along later and decides a limping girl is easy game.'

Dee's mouth tightened. 'Very funny. You're just trying to scare me.'

'No *just* about it,' he drawled back. 'I only hope I'm succeeding.'

He was, but then he hadn't really needed to try. Dee had enough imagination herself.

For his part, Baxter Ross wondered what he was going to do with her. If he had any sense, he would take her to a hospital then go.

He tried ignoring her. It was impossible. Her teeth were chattering too loudly.

'Have you no jacket?' he asked.

'It got caught on a nail,' she replied defensively. 'You must have seen it.'

He shook his head, then qualified, 'Your dog was tearing and worrying at something when I arrived. I thought it was an old rag.'

'Great,' Dee muttered, now jacketless, and wondered if the day could get any worse.

She was holding that thought when he suddenly pulled into the entrance of a deserted factory, and she tensed, hand automatically reaching for the door.

'Sit tight.' He shrugged out of his own jacket, a cracked, brown leather affair that had seen years of service. 'Put it on.' He dumped it in her lap.

Dee wanted to dump it back, but then realised how childish that action would seem.

She tried to stop her teeth chattering, knowing it was nerves as much as cold, but when she couldn't she put the jacket on rather than seem more absurd. It was heavy and worn and smelt of him.

'Right,' he said before restarting the car, 'any idea which is the nearest Casualty?'

Dee looked out of the window. They were not far from Newhouse underground. She remembered seeing signs for a St Thomas's.

Baxter used his mobile phone to call up the hospital and was warned the casualty department was operative but overstretched, and currently handling only emergencies.

He relayed all this to Dee, at the same time checking his watch.

Dee read the time on the car clock. It was well after eleven. She realised she was becoming a major inconvenience to him.

'Look, my knee has stopped hurting,' she lied, 'and I don't fancy sitting around Casualty for hours on end. So why don't we just call it a night and you drive me back to my squat?'

'Not really an option.' He offered her a look that just might have been apologetic. 'I had to take down all the boarding at the window before I could get your dog to jump out.'

'Great.' A gaping window gave her no security at all. 'Where am I meant to go now?'

'We'll worry about that in the morning,' he dismissed. 'At present a hotel would be the best bet.'

'You think I'm going to a hotel with you?' Dee made a scathing sound. 'Stroll on, mate.'

'You think I want to go to bed with you?' he countered bluntly. 'Don't flatter yourself… Separate rooms, on separate floors if you like. I won't be doing any night wandering.'

His tone told her she was as far from his taste as she could get. Dee had forgotten. She felt her face redden.

'I can't afford a hotel.' She stated the obvious.

'Just as well I can, then,' he replied, with a mocking undercurrent, and started the engine again. 'Any preference?'

Dee didn't know the name of any local hotel. 'How about the Continental?' she replied.

It wasn't a serious suggestion. She didn't imagine for one moment he was going to take her to a posh place in central London.

But he smiled briefly before calling her bluff. 'Yes, why not? If they have any rooms left… You'll find the number on their bill in my wallet.'

Dee pulled a face and cast a glance down at her torn jeans and soiled T-shirt. 'I don't think I'm quite dressed for the Mayfair Continental, do you?'

He shrugged. 'I doubt they have a dress code… The wallet's in the inside pocket.' He waited for Dee to draw it out. 'You make the call if you like, ensure I don't request adjoining rooms.'

Lazy blue eyes mocked any fears she might yet have. But, no, Dee had already received the message, loud and clear. Even if she were the last woman on earth, he would pass. Was it just her youth? Or did he find her basically unattractive? It might be reassuring but it was hardly flattering.

Scowling, she took the mobile from his hand and dug out his wallet from inside his jacket. It wasn't the most organised of affairs. She pulled out a clump of receipts and found the hotel bill among credit card slips. She did a double take at the amount. 'How many weeks were you staying at this joint?'

'Three days,' he informed her. 'It is fairly central.'

And hugely expensive. Dee rolled her eyes with disapproval, before saying, 'Are you rich or something?'

'Or something,' he replied dryly. 'After two years in the African bush, I like to treat myself to life's little luxuries.'

Put like that, it didn't sound unreasonable. Dee, however, didn't want him spending his money on her.

'Look, I was just joking about the Continental,' she ran on. 'Anywhere will do me. A bed and breakfast. As long as there's somewhere for Henry.'

'Trying to save my money for me?' he asked with a half-smile.

'Well, I don't imagine you earn a huge amount, working for a charity,' she commented bluntly.

'True,' he agreed, 'but I can still run to another night at the Continental, and we're already going in that direction so you might as well dial them.'

Dee did as requested, but when a snooty voice said, 'Continental,' she handed the mobile over to him.

Briefly Baxter Ross explained that he had checked out that morning but found he needed to stay in London for another night. He requested two singles, then two doubles, but from the conversation that ensued they clearly didn't have either.

'Yes, okay, that'll do.' He agreed to some alternative after they'd confirmed that a dog could be accommodated and rang off.

Dee waited for him to explain the arrangements. When he didn't, her doubts resurfaced.

What was she doing, letting a total stranger take her to a hotel for the night? After all, what was in it for him?

He'd made it clear he no longer wanted her to pose as a blushing bride. He'd also made it clear he disapproved of her and her lifestyle—if you could call living in a squat a lifestyle. So what did he have to gain, forking out for a hotel room?

Nothing. Unless, of course, it was the obvious thing and he did want to sleep with her?

She studied his profile as he drove through the lit-up streets of the capital. He really was remarkably good-looking, mature and tanned and fit. Most women would find him attractive.

That he'd left her thinking he was gay when they first met suggested a total confidence in his real sexuality. Perhaps he was used to effortless success with women. Perhaps he took it for granted that he could seduce her if he chose.

She was still debating the matter when they arrived at the hotel.

'All they have left is a suite,' Baxter Ross finally got round to explaining. 'But don't start panicking. I'm not proposing we share it. I'll help you register, pay your bill in advance, then go find another hotel for myself. Okay?'

'Okay,' Dee echoed, but in a tone that said she was waiting for the catch.

There was none. He did exactly what he'd said—left his own luggage in the car with Henry, shouldered her rucksack and carried her flute case in one hand, helped her up the steps with the other—no doorman barred her way this time—then hung around long enough to settle the bill.

If the desk manager had any curiosity about Dee, he kept it well hidden. He was scrupulously polite, issuing an instruction to a porter to take what little luggage she had up to her suite.

His expression didn't change when Baxter said, 'I wonder if you could possibly ring round some hotels and find a bed for me, too?'

'Certainly, sir, although it may be difficult, being the summer season,' the manager warned.

'Well, do your best,' Baxter requested with an unworried smile.

It was Dee who was frowning. What if he couldn't get anywhere?

'I'll escort you to the lift.' Baxter handed Dee her plastic security key and walked through the lobby with her. 'Your gear should already be up in your room. I'll fetch Henry. They have an indoor kennel behind the kitchens... Will you be all right?' His glance shifted to her leg.

Dee nodded. The knee was hurting like hell, but for her own reasons she didn't want him looking at it. She felt stiflingly hot in the hotel, and remembered she was still wearing his jacket.

'Here.' She started to take it off.

'Have you another one?'

'No.'

'Then keep it.'

Dee didn't argue. She needed some sort of jacket if she was going to survive the streets.

He made to offer her some money, too, but Dee didn't accept it. 'You don't have to do anything more. I'll get by.'

She tried to sound tough. Perhaps she managed it, because he nodded, 'Fair enough,' and would have gone if some impulse hadn't made her call him back.

'Baxter?' She used his name for once.

He turned in mild surprise. 'Yes?'

He waited for her to speak. If she didn't, he would be on his way.

'It's late. What if you can't get a room anywhere?' Dee found herself saying.

He seemed unconcerned. 'I'll probably drive through the night to Scotland.'

'Right.' She made a face and ran on, 'Look, this is silly. If I have a suite, that means there's two rooms. One of us could take the couch, surely?'

He frowned, and didn't exactly leap at the suggestion. In fact, he was so long in answering, Dee wondered if he thought *she* had some designs on *his* virtue.

'What's brought this on?' he asked at length. 'I thought you didn't trust me.'

'I don't trust anyone,' Dee threw back. 'But I imagine if you were planning to murder me or whatever you could have done that back at the squat, couldn't you?'

'With terrifying ease,' he agreed, with a warning in his voice, then added, 'Okay, I'll toss you for the sofa.'

A slanting smile invited her to forget their differences.

Dee knew if she didn't he would just shrug and go. This man was no threat to her.

'No way,' she responded quickly, 'the bed's mine. After three months on a floor, I deserve it.'

'All right.' He didn't argue the point but pressed the button to call the lift. 'I'll be up in about ten minutes.'

She said, 'Fine,' but she was already having second thoughts.

He misread her troubled expression. 'Is it your leg?'

'Yes.' It wasn't a total lie. The pain in her leg was a constant, dull throb, suggesting she'd pulled, strained or torn something.

'Right, I'll come up with you and take a look,' he said as the lift arrived.

Dee might have argued if she'd been given the chance. Instead a hand guided her into the lift and stayed on her arm when they got out and walked the length of a corridor.

Their suite was on the top floor. He used the key and held open the door for her. The scent of flowers hit her as she limped into the room.

Dee saw the roses first, then the bottle of champagne and glasses. Her eyes travelled over the decor and she observed aloud, 'It's the bridal suite.'

He nodded. 'It was a cancellation. I assume some couple never made it as far as the altar.'

'They probably came to their senses just in time,' Dee suggested in humourless tones.

He still smiled. 'Such cynicism in one so young.'

'Thanks.' She took it as a compliment.

Baxter laughed despite himself. She was quick, this girl-woman. Stoic, too. Pain crossed her face but she said nothing.

He switched automatically into doctor mode. 'Go into the bedroom and slip off your jeans. I'll take your bag through.'

'What?' She looked at him with wary eyes.

'The bed will be higher than this sofa, and your jeans are too tight to roll up,' he pointed out matter-of-factly.

'Right.' Dee nodded, feeling foolish. Make any fuss and she would seem even sillier.

She limped towards the bedroom. It was too richly furnished for her taste.

She perched on the bed, took off the leather jacket first, then her trainers and socks. She was just easing off the jeans when he came in to examine her.

He was unembarrassed, but then he probably spent his life seeing women in various states of undress. He knelt beside her and helped pull the jeans down her injured leg.

Baxter scrutinised her briefly. Her leg was long and slim, apart from the knee, which was painfully swollen. He manipulated it carefully, but she still bit on her lip to stop crying out.

'Badly bruised but not broken. Possibly some tendon damage, however,' he diagnosed. 'If the hotel can supply a bandage, I'll strap it up for now. An X-ray will tell us more in the morning.'

'Okay, thanks.' Dee accepted the verdict without argument.

He rose to his feet, eyes now on her face. 'I'll try to locate some painkillers, too... Are you allergic to anything?'

Dee shook her head and resisted the urge to drag on her jeans. His impersonal tones told her he viewed her simply as a patient. She was the one conscious of the sex difference.

'Meanwhile, lie down and take the pressure off the knee,' he instructed, already pulling back the covers so Dee could slip inside the bed.

He helped lift up her leg, and when she lay down draped a fine linen sheet over her.

'Thanks.' It was so cool Dee's teeth started to chatter again.

He put a hand to her brow, as if feeling for fever. 'Hang on. I'll be back soon.'

Dee nodded. She wasn't going anywhere. She felt drained, as if this day had lasted a week.

She listened to the doors shut behind him, then lay on her side. She caught her reflection in a wardrobe mirror.

She looked gaunt and unkempt. It had been months since she'd slept in a proper bed, longer since she'd slept without fear.

Tomorrow she would be faced with a choice. Back to the streets, and loneliness, and a life that was no real life at all. Or home once more to the bosom of her family and the hope that Edward would leave her alone. Two choices, but neither seemed tolerable tonight.

She shut her eyes. She was too tired for decisions now. So tired, even the throbbing in her knee wasn't going to keep her awake. She was beyond tired, in fact, in a state of witless exhaustion.

Baxter found her asleep, curled up in a foetal position, the light still on. He put the painkillers and bandage on the bedside cabinet. They would keep until tomorrow.

He sat carefully on the bed and touched her forehead with the back of his hand. Her skin was warm, damp even, but there was no real temperature, he judged.

He watched her for a moment. She was different in sleep. Long lashes created shadows on pale cheeks and hid the glass-hard eyes. Her lips were moving slightly, as if she was dreaming. With the sneer gone, her mouth was soft and full. Even the ruthless haircut couldn't hide it. This girl-woman would one day be beautiful...

Assuming she lived that long.

CHAPTER FOUR

DEE woke in the night and found Baxter Ross standing over her. He was naked to the waist, his body illuminated by a bedside lamp. She stared at him in confusion; she'd been dreaming of a man, but not this one.

'It's all right,' he assured her as her eyes became fearful. 'I'm not going to harm you. I heard you crying. I thought you might be in pain.'

Dee took a moment to focus on what he was saying. Crying? Yes; she felt the tears on her cheek. It wasn't the first time.

She moved her leg and found she *was* in pain, so she grimaced. Let him think that was what had caused her tears.

'I'll get you something.' He moved out of range.

Dee heard a tap running in the bathroom and pulled herself into a sitting position. He returned with a glass of water.

'Here.' He handed her the glass, then shook out a couple of pills from a bottle on the bedside cabinet. 'They're just paracetamol, but they should take the edge off the pain.'

'Thanks.' She gulped the water and pills down. Maybe it *was* the pain that had brought on the nightmare this time. 'I'm sorry if I woke you.'

'I wasn't asleep.' He took the glass from her hand and added, 'May I examine your leg?'

His formal tone contrasted with the intimacy of their situation. If Dee didn't trust him, she understood she could just say no.

She nodded warily.

He shifted just enough of the sheet to expose her lower leg. His hands moved with cool efficiency on her inflamed skin.

'You have fluid on the knee,' he eventually declared. 'I'll

bandage it in the morning for support, but it'll have to be drained.'

'Great.'

'It won't be too bad.'

Dee was sceptical. 'How do you know? Have you had it done?'

'Not exactly,' he admitted, 'but I've done it a few times.'

She pulled a face. 'Different perspective, wouldn't you say?'

'Perhaps,' he conceded.

Dee actually knew what she was talking about. She'd had it drained before, and it wasn't an experience she was in a hurry to repeat.

She switched to asking, 'Was Henry all right?'

'Seemed it. I left him wolfing down kitchen scraps,' he relayed with a slight smile.

Dee still felt a measure of guilt, having gone to sleep without checking. She supposed she must have trusted Baxter Ross to take care of things.

She trusted him now, too, as, exhausted, she lay back down on her pillows.

Baxter ran a practised eye over her. In this light she looked anaemic and badly nourished. Not to the extent of his African patients, but on the road there.

He lifted her wrist from the bed and took her pulse.

Dee was unable to object. His interest was purely professional.

She was the one conscious of him, of the surprisingly calloused forefinger pressing on her vein, the muscular arm flexed so he could read his watch. His chest was broad and covered in bronzed hair tapering down to his waist. He was so masculine, the sense of him was overpowering.

It came almost as a shock. After Edward, she'd imagined herself dead to certain emotions. Yet here she was, physically attracted to a man who wouldn't notice her if she were stark naked. That had to be perverse.

'Your pulse is rapid,' he finally commented.

Dee coloured, though it seemed unlikely he would know why. He was quite immune to her.

'That's normal for me,' she claimed rather foolishly.

His frown deepened. 'Perhaps you need a general check-up.'

'No, thanks!' Dee didn't want to discover any more peculiar feelings.

'Not by me.' He gave a brief smile at her rapid refusal. 'That really would be straining my code of ethics.'

'Oh.' Dee wondered what he meant by that.

'I probably shouldn't have come in here as it is,' he added dryly. 'So, unless there's anything else, I'll disappear.'

'No, I'm fine,' Dee assured him.

He nodded, then stretched a bare arm out to the light. 'Off or on?'

'Off.' Dee had no fear of the dark, just her dreams. She waited until he was at the door before saying, 'Thanks, Doc.'

It wasn't much. Gratitude didn't come easily to her. But it was sincere enough.

His voice came back to her in the darkness. 'No problem.' It was a quiet understatement before he slipped out of the room.

Dee knew better, of course. In his eyes, she *was* a problem. Incapacitated. No longer useful to him. Chances were he would be gone in the morning.

Dee drifted back to sleep as the painkillers kicked in. This time there were no dreams, good or bad, and, wrapped in the luxury of the huge queen-size bed, she could have slept the clock around.

She was woken instead by the sound of knocking and her name being called. She tried ignoring both.

Baxter Ross came in anyway, asking from the doorway, 'Dee, are you awake?'

'No,' Dee grunted, and pulled a pillow over her head as he crossed to draw the curtains and let a flood of light into the room.

He came back to stand by her bed. 'How are you?'

Dee emerged reluctantly from behind her pillow.

Dishevelled, crusty-eyed and not particularly clean—that was how she was.

Whereas he was immaculate in cotton chinos and a khaki-coloured shirt. There was no sign that he had been up till late.

'Fine,' she lied as she tried to sit up and jarred her knee in the process.

'I don't think so.' He drew the sheet away to take a look at her leg.

Dee hastily pushed down her T-shirt from around her middle so it at least covered her pants. Not that he was interested or embarrassed.

'Mmm...I'll strap it up for now, but I think we should get it X-rayed.' He picked up a rolled bandage from the bedside cabinet and unravelled it.

Dee wondered about this 'we' business. She'd half expected him to be gone by now. Still, she didn't argue.

'Can I take a shower first?' she asked.

'Sure.' He offered her a hand.

Dee tried to make it on her own, but more than her knee seemed to have stiffened up. She would have stumbled had he not gripped her arm.

'Sorry,' she muttered, at her helplessness.

'No need to be.' He supported her to the bathroom and set her down on the closed toilet seat. 'I think it'll have to be a bath.'

'That's fine.' Dee meant for him to go.

Instead he put in the plug and ran the water for her. 'How do you like it?'

'Hot, please.' She watched the steaming water cascade into the bath, and murmured aloud, 'Luxury.'

He smiled quizzically, 'Having your bath run?'

'No, having a bath.' She smiled back.

'Of course.' He turned off the taps and leaned back against the door, giving her breathing space.

'You can get in the bath by yourself?' He clearly wasn't anxious to help her.

She nodded.

'Right, I'll leave you to it.' He straightened and went out of the bathroom door.

Dee realised she had no need to lock it. His lack of interest in her was so obvious, it was almost insulting. In fact, there was no 'almost' about it, she decided, glancing in a mirror and wincing herself at the sight of hollow eyes in a face too gaunt even for fashion. Would he have liked her before, when her hair had been long and her skin had been glowing with health?

Dee shook her head at her thoughts. What did his opinion matter, anyway?

It took effort to lever herself down into the bath, but it was worth it. For five minutes she just wallowed. Then, avoiding the swollen knee, she scrubbed at four days' dirt, emptied out the bath and refilled it, and scrubbed again until she was pink and shiny.

She finally emerged into the bedroom with a bath towel wrapped round her body like a sarong.

Dee had assumed he would be in the other room. Instead he was waiting for her here, seated in an armchair. He turned from an uninspiring view of the London skyline and looked at her briefly, not long enough to make Dee feel uncomfortable.

Some of the stiffness had gone from her leg, and she managed to hobble over to her rucksack. She found clean underwear and a coral T-shirt and slipped them on while he contemplated the view once more.

She made sure the T-shirt covered her modesty before saying, 'Could you strap my leg, please?'

'Sure. Sit on the bed.'

He sat beside her and wound the bandage round her knee, tight enough for support but without constricting the blood flow. Any pain Dee kept to herself.

'Not the neatest of jobs.' He appraised his own work as he finally inserted a safety pin to hold the layers together. 'Bandaging isn't my line of expertise.'

'Feels good to me,' she said, with a hint of gratitude.

He glanced up at her before replying, 'Well, you're a good patient. Very uncomplaining... How long have you been living rough, by the way?'

It sounded like a *non-sequitur,* but Dee followed his train of thought. He assumed—rightly—that life on the streets had toughened her up.

'Three months this time,' she admitted.

'This time?' he echoed.

'I went home the first time my money ran out.' Her lips twisted, indicating it had been a mistake.

It had also been a mistake telling him. 'You *can* go home?' he queried.

Yes, if I want to be molested, she could have said, but didn't. What business was it of his?

He read her silence as assent, and went on, 'So, why don't you? Home can surely be no worse than your current existence?'

'That's all you know!' She flicked him a dismissive look before edging to the other side of the bed. She took her jeans with her and dragged them on over the bandaging, then stood to zip them and buckle her belt. She was too angry now to be self-conscious.

Baxter Ross waited till she'd finished to say, 'Tell me, then.'

'Use your imagination!' She turned her back on him and threw her dirty clothes in the rucksack. She tied the top, shouldered it and picked up her flute case. It all took an effort, though his bandaging seemed to have made her more mobile.

She walked to the door. It was to have been a grand exit, only with her hands full she couldn't manage to unlock the door.

Baxter walked up behind her. She thought he meant to help, but instead he took the rucksack from her hand.

'Don't be silly. You won't be able to manage more than a few hundred yards with that lot.'

Talked to as if she were a child, Dee responded accordingly. 'Why should you care?'

His brows gathered into a frown, as if he was really considering the question.

'I probably don't,' he admitted at length. 'It just strikes me as crazy, you limping off into the sunset when you could have breakfast first. I've already paid for it so you might as well eat it.'

Dee's pride did silent battle with hunger. Pride lost.

'Yeah, okay, if you want.' She made it sound as if she was doing him the favour.

Baxter Ross let it pass. She had a lot of attitude for a girl in her situation, but maybe she needed it to survive.

'Afterwards I'll drop you off at the hospital.' He took her bags from her and, leaving them on a luggage rack, opened the door for her.

Dee limped through to the sitting room. She hadn't quite taken in the suite's decor last night. Two huge bouquets of flowers rested on highly polished tables while heavily draped windows in cream and floral satin matched a deep plush sofa. Fit for a bride on her wedding night.

Dee caught her reflection in a gilt-edged mirror. She looked like an alien in this romantic setting. Not that she cared—she didn't believe in hearts and flowers and happy-ever-afters.

She glanced at the sofa again. If Baxter Ross had slept there, there was no indication of it. Perhaps he'd just sat within arm's reach of the complimentary champagne, which now lay open in its bucket alongside a solitary glass.

Was he a drinker? He'd seemed sober last night, and wasn't hung-over now, but what did that mean? Maybe hardened drinkers didn't get drunk on a single bottle.

'Anything wrong?' He caught her troubled expression.

Dee told herself his drinking habits weren't her concern, and confined herself to a meaningful, 'I see you enjoyed the champagne.'

Baxter had to laugh. There was such an obvious sniff of disapproval in her voice.

She rounded on him. 'What's so funny?'

'You sound like my dear old grandmother,' he drawled, 'about to warn me off the demon drink.'

Dee still didn't consider it amusing. 'Perhaps you need warning,' she said in repressive tones.

He laughed again, refusing to take offence. 'Possibly, but if it's all the same to you I'll find a grown-up to do it,' was his dry comment as he crossed to the outer door and held it open for her.

Dee understood well enough. He thought she was just a

kid, but she wasn't. She proved it to herself by limping past him, head held high.

He fell in step beside her as they walked down the corridor, but she studiously ignored him, and shrugged off the supportive hand he tried to give her.

'You're not sulking with me, are you?' he asked as they descended in the lift.

'No,' she bit back, 'I'm fuming. There's a difference.'

'Right.' Baxter knew better than to laugh this time, but it was hard to take her too seriously. 'Look, I'm sorry if I've upset you. It's just that you seem rather young to be dispensing advice.'

Dee gave him a superior look from her corner of the lift. 'Everything's relative. I'm sure I do seem young to *you*,' she stressed.

He didn't have to be Einstein to work out the insult, but just laughed. 'One all. I think we could call it quits, don't you?'

'I suppose.' Dee shrugged, but still didn't let him help her limp to the dining room. She was going to have to stand on her own two feet soon enough.

Being the last down to breakfast, they drew interested stares from several of the other guests. Perhaps they looked an odd couple—Baxter Ross, so clean-cut and smart even in casual clothes, her in her ripped jeans, T-shirt and Doc Martens.

It was also the kind of posh hotel where waiters looked down their noses at anyone 'common'. The one who served them glanced briefly at Dee, then directed all his questions to Baxter Ross.

'Am I invisible or something?' she muttered, when the waiter had departed.

Baxter Ross raised an ironic brow. 'Actually, no. I'd say you're probably the most visible person in this room right at the moment.'

His eyes rested on her hedgehog style hair and the three gold earrings that adorned her left earlobe.

Dee supposed she looked unfeminine to him, but that was the idea. Look tough and hopefully people took you for tough and didn't mess you around.

She caught the eye of some dress-up doll-type at a nearby table and openly stared back until the woman turned away.

Baxter observed the little interplay, and said dryly, 'Well, I think you managed to scare the life out of her.'

'Silly cow,' Dee muttered back, and was given a reproving frown. 'I bet she's just your type—all teeth, hair and helplessness.'

'Not particularly,' he denied evenly.

'So what is?' she flipped back.

He shrugged, as if he'd never thought about it, then responded, 'I like good-looking women. Who doesn't? But no specific type. So long as they're intelligent, mature and independent.'

'Career women,' Dee summed up from this list.

He nodded. 'Mostly.'

She wrinkled her nose in response.

'I take it that doesn't meet with your approval?' he concluded.

It certainly put Dee well out of the running. Not that she'd wanted to be in it or anything.

'Sounds terminal to me,' she commented. 'But what do I know?'

Terminally boring, Baxter Ross was left to conclude for himself.

'Quite,' he agreed. 'What *do* you know?'

He levelled her a look that suggested she was hardly a world expert on life and how it should be lived.

Dee was undaunted. 'Well, you haven't found Mrs Right yet, have you? Otherwise you wouldn't have to pick up strange girls in underground stations so you can fulfil some old dear's wishes.'

'Really?' Baxter wondered if it was too late for the truth. Perhaps. She seemed quite happy with the nonsense she herself had made up yesterday. He confined himself to a murmur. '"Strange" being the operative word.'

Dee pulled a face back at him, before musing, 'She probably meant well. I mean she probably felt you should be married by now, being the age you are and everything, and wanted to give you an incentive to get on with it.'

Baxter didn't know whether to be annoyed or amused by this reasoning.

He was still deciding which to be when she added, 'It's still a fairly quirky thing to do—unless, of course, she already had a candidate in mind.'

'Candidate?' he echoed, trailing slightly behind this creative flow.

'For the job of Mrs Baxter Ross,' she said with an impatient edge.

'Right.' He nodded, although she wasn't remotely right.

'Did she, then?' Dee prompted when he failed to be more forthcoming.

'Possibly.' Baxter found himself entering her fantasy rather than disillusion her. 'There have been women, but my relationships tend to founder for logistical reasons.'

'What?' Dee asked inelegantly.

'I've been based in Africa ten months of each year,' he explained. 'You can't expect women to wait around in those circumstances.'

Something in his voice, a certain insouciance, had Dee returning, 'Have you ever asked one to?'

She was quick. Baxter had to give her that.

'As a matter of fact,' he drawled back, 'no, I haven't.'

Because the women had just been recreation, Dee supposed. Part of his leave, before he went back to the fray. Had the women known that?

He seemed to read her mind, or perhaps just her critical expression, as he added, 'I have never been dishonest about my intentions with any woman.'

'Doesn't stop them hoping, though,' she commented. Before he imagined this was a personal observation, she added, 'Who knows? Maybe one of them might volunteer for marriage duty.'

'I doubt it.' He smiled at the idea. 'My last girlfriend has just become a chief medical adviser for the World Health Organization, so I imagine a marriage of convenience would have minimal appeal. And her predecessor is currently dating the heir to a Scottish earldom, as well as being heavily involved in the Edinburgh Festival. I think life has moved on for both of them.'

He sounded wry rather than regretful. It was Dee who was left wishing she'd never started this conversation. Had she really needed to know his type was clever, talented, successful women who made her seem a complete no-hoper?

'Whereas you figured I was desperate,' she concluded for herself.

He shrugged rather than give her a direct answer, but it was obvious. It was true, too. Given the chance, Dee suspected she might still agree to his scheme. What other options had she?

Breakfast arrived, and she abandoned further conversation. She'd ordered the full works—sausage, bacon, egg et cetera. It was nearly two days since she'd had a proper meal; in fact, hc'd bought the last one, too. She tried to eat slower this time, but it was hard not to wolf it down.

Baxter recognised her hunger from the way she was eating. He wondered what he should do for her. He could give her money, but God alone knew if she'd spend it wisely. He could pay for her to stay in a hotel for a couple of weeks and hope she might find work in the interim. That, of course, was assuming she wanted work.

He asked her later, on the way to the hospital. 'What sort of job would you like? One you could realistically get.'

She caught his drift. 'Besides rocket scientist and brain surgeon, you mean? I don't know, Doc. You tell me what job I'd like and could get that doesn't require things such as references and home addresses.'

'I didn't say it would be easy.' Baxter wondered if she was right. Was it impossible for someone in her situation to get a job? 'Perhaps if you tried for a more conventional appearance...' he suggested. 'I could buy you some clothes—a skirt suit, perhaps.'

'Great idea.' Dee rolled her eyes heavenwards. 'Then people would think you're my sugar daddy.'

Baxter was glad he didn't expect gratitude from this girl.

'Thanks for telling me. I hadn't realised I'd slipped into that age category,' he replied dryly.

'It's nothing personal. I just don't like taking charity. Last night was enough.'

'Where are you going to stay tonight? I understand your last place is about to be demolished.'

'Haven't thought about it.' Dee didn't want to depress herself by considering her limited options.

'You don't sound worried,' he concluded from her tone.

She shrugged. 'There's always somewhere.'

Shop doorways. Parks. A different squat.

'Here we are.' He drew up at the casualty department of a hospital, coming round to open her door and help her out of the car. 'You go inside. I'll park.'

'I thought you were just dropping me off.' Dee had assumed as much.

'And leave Old Faithful tied to a railing?' A glance took in the dog, slumbering in the boot. 'Your choice.'

'No, I... I...' Dee forced it out. 'I'd be grateful if you could wait.'

She didn't like asking him for anything. Baxter understood that, but he didn't make capital out of it.

'Okay, go to the desk and give your name. Ask for Sister Sullivan,' he told her. 'I'll follow you in.'

'Sister Sullivan?'

'Someone I used to work with. She's Casualty Sister here.'

Dee nodded and watched him drive away before limping through an entrance door directly into a waiting area. It was early so there were few 'customers' as yet.

She gave her name at the desk, then said uncertainly, 'I'm to ask for Sister Sullivan.'

The receptionist frowned, and Dee half expected her to deny the existence of such a person. Instead she gave a nod, then, handing her a form to complete, told Dee to take a seat.

Dee had only a minute or two to wait before a nurse in a sister's uniform appeared. She was a pretty woman of about thirty, with dark hair in a French plait.

'Baxter's friend?' she enquired with some doubt.

'Sort of,' Dee conceded. 'He said I should ask for you. He's just gone to park his car.'

'Right, follow me.' The woman smiled, leading Dee past Reception to a free cubicle.

Dee was given a gown, and was changed by the time a doctor appeared. He looked at the knee briefly, then ordered a porter to wheel her down for an X-ray.

When she returned she found Baxter sitting at the nurses' station with Sister Sullivan. Their heads were close and they were laughing at some joke, friendship quickly re-established. What kind of friendship? Dee wondered, a tight knot suddenly in her stomach as she was wheeled past them to wait alone in the cubicle until the duty doctor was free.

Baxter appeared at her side only when the young medic arrived. The latter took the envelope that had been handed to her in Radiology and, slipping out her X-ray, held it to the light. He obviously knew who Baxter was as they discussed her injury.

In fact, it was Baxter who directed a question at her. 'Why didn't you say you'd injured the knee previously?'

She shrugged. 'You didn't ask.'

His eyes narrowed at her flippant attitude, before he asked the junior, 'How do you propose treating the knee?'

'Drain and strap?' he suggested with a questioning lift of his eyebrows.

Baxter nodded in agreement. 'Any chance of admitting her, too? Run some tests on her general state of health? At the very least, she's anaemic.'

'I doubt there's bed space,' the young doctor replied, 'but I could check.'

'I am not staying!' Dee refused point-blank as the other man departed.

'We'll see,' Baxter Ross responded. 'Meanwhile, when and how did you damage the knee first time around?'

'A year ago,' she shrugged, and relayed succinctly, 'I fell down some stairs.'

He raised a brow. 'You seem to make a habit of this. Who was chasing you that time?'

'No one.' Just her own private demons.

'Well, you'll have to start nursing that leg,' he advised, 'unless you want a permanent injury.'

'I'm not staying in hospital,' Dee repeated stubbornly.

He shook his head at her refusal. 'You're being irrational. You have to rest that leg somehow, and that's hardly possible if you're dragging a dog around the London underground while you beg for a living.'

'I *busk*,' Dee corrected him furiously.

'All right, busk,' he sighed at her touchiness. 'Whichever, that leg is going to limit your mobility. Even you must see that.'

Even her? It was a telling phrase.

'You think I'm stupid, don't you?' Her face was tight with anger.

'I didn't say that. You're clearly not stupid. You're just.…well, very young,' he added, as if only just realising it.

Concerned eyes rested on Dee, and for once she didn't have a snappy reply. She knew she was young. She wanted to be—young, carefree, with a whole life of possibilities stretching out before her. She just didn't feel it any more.

'You're not even eighteen, are you?' he judged, despite the dark shadows above the hollow cheeks.

Dee decided not to lie. 'I am almost.'

He shook his head, disapproval evident.

He didn't get a chance to express it, however, as the houseman returned with a tray of instruments and a nurse to assist him.

Dee almost passed out when she saw the size of the drainage needle. Luckily a smaller needle was used to numb the area first.

Then Baxter and the younger medic conferred on the best site from which to drain her knee.

'Thanks.' The houseman accepted Baxter's advice before admitting candidly, 'I haven't done many of these.'

He hadn't done any, Dee suspected, beginning to feel like a guinea pig as he approached with the needle, and she looked away again.

Baxter Ross appeared at the other side of the bed, saying nothing, but he took her hand and she squeezed it hard while the business was done. It helped, giving her the brief impression that she wasn't going through the whole thing alone, but when the procedure was over they both withdrew from the contact.

The young doctor congratulated her on keeping still, then, shaking hands with Baxter, departed with a satisfied air.

The nurse was left to bandage up Dee's knee while Baxter looked silently on.

'That's it.' She straightened from the task and smiled. 'We can get you dressed now, lovey.'

She must have imagined Dee and Baxter were intimate because she reached round to the back of Dee's hospital gown and began to untie the strings there.

Slow to realise her intention, Dee was left to clutch the gown to her breasts. She was naked but for her briefs.

Baxter had a view of her surprisingly shapely back before drawling, 'I think I'll make myself scarce.'

Dee heard what could have been amusement in his voice. Perhaps that wasn't surprising. She had no need for modesty. In his role as a doctor, he had probably seen thousands of women's breasts.

Dee held onto the gown until the nurse fetched her clothes from the chair. She was pulling her T-shirt over her head when Sister Sullivan slipped through the cubicle curtains to relieve the other nurse.

'I shouldn't put on any more,' she advised. 'Dr Roper's trying to find you a bed.'

'Why?' Dee knew her injury didn't require hospitalisation. 'I'm sure I can walk.'

'Nevertheless, Doctor feels it might be wise to run some tests on your general state of health,' the senior nurse explained.

'You mean Baxter does.' Dee guessed who had been the instigator. 'Well, no, thanks. He just wants to make me someone else's problem.'

Sister Sullivan frowned at the comment, before continuing, 'Not at all. I'm sure he has your best interests at heart, and I really think you should heed his advice.'

Dee shook her head. 'I can't. I have commitments... So could someone help me on with my jeans please?'

Her tone was insistent but the sister ignored it, saying,

'We'll see what the doctor says first, shall we?' and slipping out of the cubicle.

She didn't go far. Dee heard her outside, talking to Baxter. She caught the words, 'Who is this girl really?'

And the amused rejoinder, 'No one, just a waif and stray I've picked up.'

Dee heard the woman laugh and, face aflame, she reached for her jeans and tried to drag them on herself.

'What are you doing?' Baxter barked at her when he entered the cubicle to find her dressing.

'Getting out of here,' she retorted, struggling to get the jeans material past the bulge of her bandage.

'Lie back!' He came over and half pushed her back on the trolley.

He was oblivious to her state of undress. It was Dee who felt utterly conscious of him as he eased the jeans carefully past her damaged knee, then lifted her hips slightly to slide them under her bottom.

'You really are too thin. Your hip bones are jutting out of your pelvis,' he commented, strictly from a medical angle.

'It's the waif look!' she threw back, and pushed his hands away when he would have drawn up her jeans' zip.

'You heard what I was saying to Cathy Sullivan.' He threw her an apologetic glance.

Dee ignored it, in no mood to be pacified. She sat up again and swung her legs over the side of the trolley. She had some idea of hopping to the floor, but he was standing in her way.

'I think you should consider admission,' he resumed in patient tones. 'Let them run a few blood tests. At the very least you're anaemic.'

'Forget it,' Dee dismissed. 'I don't need blood tests. I just want to get out of here.'

She tried to get off the examination trolley but he barred her way. 'On one condition.'

Dee wanted to tell him to stuff his conditions, but she felt powerless. Even if she created a scene, it wouldn't be her that the nurses and doctors outside would support.

'What?' she seethed in frustration.

'You refuse to stay here, and yet you can't possibly take care of yourself.' He declared. 'So either you go to Scotland with me or you go home.'

'*What?*' she demanded, incredulous now. 'You still want me to marry you?'

He hesitated before shaking his head. 'No, I think that was one of my crazier ideas, but I imagine I could put up with you for a few weeks while you recuperate.'

Charity, in other words. But what else was there? Home? Where the heart certainly wasn't. She'd be on sufferance in either case.

'I'll go home,' she finally said in resigned tones.

'Good.' His relief was evident as he helped her down.

Dee understood. He hadn't wanted her, of course. He had made the offer because he felt he had to.

Well, what else had she expected? Her own family didn't want her. Well, her mother didn't.

She thought of that last time at home—Edward's arms round her, his wet mouth on hers, hands pulling at her clothes, words spilling out over her protests.

She remembered veering between fear and disgust, pushing at his shoulders while he pushed up her skirt. She remembered the bile in her throat as he panted his love for her. *He* had wanted her—hadn't he just!

Carried away, he hadn't heard the kitchen door open, hadn't seen her mother's face, hadn't stopped until she'd cried out, 'How could you?'

How could *he?* Dee had assumed as she'd freed herself and run to her mother's arms.

Only when Barbara Litton had repeated, 'How could you?' had Dee realised it was directed at her.

It had gone straight to her heart like a knife, severing arteries, blood ties, cutting her loose on the world.

She had never planned to go home. She didn't plan it now. She would let Baxter Ross drop her off at the railway station, duty done.

He knelt beside her to put on her socks and boots, and she felt a flicker of guilt that was extinguished as he added, 'It's probably for the best.'

The child in her wanted to scream at him then, *What do you know?* because he really didn't.

No one knew.

CHAPTER FIVE

'I AM not going home,' Dee bit out for the third time. 'Why don't you listen to me?'

'Because not ten minutes ago you said you were.'

'That was before.'

Before she'd discovered Baxter Ross was nobody's fool and intended driving her to the doorstep of her house. She'd tried to slip out of the car, but he'd snapped shut the locks from the console.

'You never planned on going, did you?'

'No.'

'Right, that leaves us with Scotland.' He switched the engine back on.

'No way!' She pulled the lock button up and this time managed to open the door.

'Do that and I'll drive off,' he threatened. 'That'll leave you bagless and dogless.'

'You wouldn't.' She couldn't believe he'd saddle himself with someone else's dog, but his expression said otherwise. 'Why are you doing this? I'm nothing to you.'

He didn't disagree. 'Call it bloody-mindedness. Now, which is it? Home or Scotland?'

'Neither.' Dee refused to let him win.

Baxter finally lost patience and stretched over to the back seat for her rucksack.

'What are you doing?' Dee demanded, although it was evident as he started emptying the contents, discarding each item into her lap. 'Give me that.'

She made a grab for the envelope he'd found in an inner pocket of the bag, but he held it out of reach. He drew out her passport and found her birth certificate in its folds.

His eyes widened as he read it. 'Your father's a doctor?'

'*Was,*' she corrected. 'He's dead.'

'And your mother's a model,' he added.

'*Was,*' she corrected again. 'She's *brain* dead.'

'So much for the little cockney sparrow act,' he dismissed. 'I suppose it gives you more street cred?'

'You try being middle class and homeless,' she threw back. 'People don't like it. They think you must be a real waste of space to have fallen that far.'

'Only you're not—homeless, that is.' He read from the certificate. 'Willow Trees, Steeple Hartdean, Near Royston, Hertfordshire. Sounds posh.'

'Terribly,' Dee sneered in agreement.

'So what's the chance of your family still living there—' he paused to check her year of birth '—seventeen years on?'

His eyes caught hers, testing her for the truth. She stared back, giving nothing away.

'No, I wouldn't think so,' he decided for himself. 'Most people move house at some time or other... Still, it's a start.'

He dumped the passport and bag on her lap and restarted the car. He seemed to know where he was going because he didn't stop to ask directions.

Dee seethed in silence for almost an hour before they reached the signs for the A1 and she realised where they were going.

'I shouldn't bother,' she finally burst out.

'She speaks.' He awarded her a brief glance. 'For a while there I thought you'd been struck dumb... What should I not bother with?'

'Going to Willow Trees,' she replied. 'My father died. My mother remarried. We moved.'

She sounded smug, feeling she'd foiled him.

Baxter kept driving, but asked, 'Which was more traumatic—the moving or the stepfather?'

'Neither. We moved to a palace and my stepfather was a prince,' she claimed in sardonic tones.

Behind them lay some truth. Her stepfather was well off, they had moved to a grander house and she'd been indulged materially.

'All right, so don't tell me.' Baxter shrugged. 'Just give me the general directions to this palace.'

Dee refused with silence.

He sighed aloud. 'We can do it the hard way, if that's what you'd prefer.'

'The hard way?'

'We go to the address on your birth certificate and I make enquiries there.'

'They'll think you're mad.' Dee had similar doubts herself.

But he was still clever. 'I'll tell them you're suffering from amnesia and theirs is the only address we have to go on.'

Dee glanced at him. He wasn't joking. The slight smile on his face was one of satisfaction. He enjoyed getting the better of her.

'Go ahead.' She decided to call his bluff.

Only he wasn't bluffing. He kept driving, getting closer and closer to Royston. And the trouble was that although Dee had moved, it had been within the same village.

They were in Royston when Baxter pulled into a filling station and took out a road map from the glove compartment.

'Okay, do you tell me where it is, or do we go down the amnesia route?'

Dee was torn. It was already noon. She would need enough daylight to allow for a slow hitch back to London.

She pointed to Steeple Hartdean on the map. 'Same village, different house.'

'Three miles or so,' he observed.

Quite, Dee thought, her stomach turning over.

Perhaps he was into mind-reading, because he asked, 'What sort of reception are you expecting?'

'Well, I don't think they'll be rushing out to kill any fatted calves,' she confided dryly.

Baxter wasn't entirely surprised. 'How long since you've been home?'

'Easter.'

'Like to tell me why you left?' he added, more casually than curiously.

'No,' she answered briefly.

Fair enough, Baxter thought, not sure if he wanted to

know. He had picked up this girl to solve a problem of his own, not to get involved in hers.

'I'm going to buy some petrol and a sandwich. Anything you want?' He nodded towards the service-station shop.

'Cigarettes?' Dee said, without much hope of getting them.

'I meant food,' he said reprovingly. 'Smoking kills, or haven't you heard?'

Dee gave him a resentful look. Did he have to sound like someone's dad all the time? He wasn't *that* old.

'So? Practically every doctor I know smokes,' she claimed rather extravagantly.

Certainly her father had smoked, and so did Edward, her stepfather. It had been his cigarettes she had first smoked in the toilet at home and, on being discovered, she had hardly been discouraged. But then it had been a sign she was growing up, and Edward had hardly been able to wait for that.

'I'm surprised you can afford to smoke,' Baxter Ross added.

'I can't,' she countered. 'And, before you read me a lecture on dole scroungers wasting their money on cigarettes, I don't qualify for benefit. If I sometimes choose to buy a packet rather than eat with my busking money, then that's *my* decision.'

In fact, Dee hadn't smoked for weeks. She just needed one now. A crutch to help her face the family reunion.

She didn't expect him to understand and, when he responded with a 'Hmm' before climbing out to fill the hire-car with petrol, she assumed her request was being denied.

But that was Baxter Ross—unpredictable. He remained grim faced even as he returned from the shop to throw a packet of cigarettes and matches in her lap.

'You're a life-saver.' Dee's smile was quick and natural for once.

'Not according to the government health warning on the packet,' he replied dryly.

Dee read it briefly, then with the barest hesitation unwrapped the cellophane. Like most young people she viewed death as so distant a prospect it was unimaginable.

She took out a cigarette, and was about to light up when he instructed, 'Wait.'

Dee frowned, not understanding, but did as she was told.

He drove to some wasteland at the rear of the service station. 'I'll give you five minutes.'

Dee caught on. He might be prepared to buy her cigarettes but he wasn't going to let her foul up his air. She climbed out of the car and pointedly leaned against the front bonnet while she lit up.

It was just as well she was leaning on something, as the first puff made her head swim. She still smoked it halfway down to the filter before stubbing it out.

He grimaced as she climbed back into the car.

'Okay, I smell like an ashtray,' she said before he could, then couldn't resist adding, 'So tell me, Doc. Does it ever get boring, being so perfect yourself?'

He got the point and laughed all the same. 'Sometimes… In fact, it can be pretty hard work.'

Dee smiled briefly, then caught herself at it. She was determined not to like this man.

'Okay, let's get this over with,' she went on, ready as she was ever going to be.

Baxter glanced towards her. She was clearly nervous. But why?

'Directions?' he requested.

Dee supplied them in a flat, spare tone until they finally reached the place where she'd spent much of her childhood. In her father's day they'd lived in a detached house in the village that had included his surgery. When her mother had married Edward, they'd moved to one of the more substantial houses on the outskirts.

The village had grown bigger over the years, but was still small enough for most people to be on nodding acquaintance. Dee sat, expressionless, as they drove past the junior school she'd attended and the church where they'd buried her father.

It was the retriever who reacted. Alerted by their slowing in speed, he sat up, looked out at the back window and, recognising something familiar, sights or smells, let out a sound that was between a bark and a howl.

Dee remained slumped in the front seat. 'Take the left fork,' she instructed Baxter Ross. 'It's about a mile down here.'

They passed the riding stables where Dee had gone as a young child, then a field or two, before they reached a mature residential area where all the houses were hidden by high walls.

Her nerve went a hundred yards short of Oakfield. 'Pull up here.'

He did as she requested. 'Have we passed it?'

'Not yet.' Now she was here, Dee recalled even more vividly why she'd left. Would anything have changed? Had the last three months made her better equipped to deal with Edward?

Baxter watched her closely, detecting anxiety—or was it fear? What might a smart-mouthed, streetwise kid like Dee be scared of?

'What's wrong?' he asked simply.

Dee shook her head. She had told the truth before and hadn't been believed. She wouldn't make that mistake again.

'I don't want to do this,' she said instead. 'Will you take me back to London?'

He shook his head. 'We're here now.'

'Look, this is a waste of time.' She said what she felt. 'They won't want to see me, so why go through the grief?'

'Maybe you're right.' Baxter could imagine she hadn't been the easiest of teenagers to control. 'But at the very least you could let them know you're still alive.'

'Trust you,' Dee muttered back.

'What's that supposed to mean?' Baxter sighed in return.

'To see things from their perspective. I suppose it's a generation thing,' she added pointedly.

Baxter was left feeling old enough to be her father.

'Quite,' he agreed, suddenly losing patience as he jammed the car into gear and revved up. 'Now, which one?' he demanded.

'First on the left, but you're not coming in.'

'Fair enough.'

Baxter had no desire to be present at the reunion. Families were, in some respects, foreign territory to him.

He turned in where she indicated and raised a brow. At the end of the drive lay a sizeable brick-built house, with a small flight of steps leading to a flagged terrace.

Dee breathed a sigh of relief. Her mother's car was there. Her stepfather's wasn't.

'You can drop me off here,' she commanded rather imperiously. 'Thanks for the lift. I can get the stuff myself.'

She pushed open the passenger door and, swinging her gammy leg out, managed to lever herself to her feet. She limped round to the boot to let out an excitedly barking Henry.

For an old dog he moved surprisingly fast, jumping across the front terrace, through a gate at the side, and round the back to familiar stomping ground.

Dee emptied the rest of her things from the car, placing them next to the miniature stone lion that guarded the steps. She lifted a hand to wave goodbye to him.

About to go, Baxter felt his eyes drawn as the front door opened and a blonde woman appeared, giving the car a quizzical look before spotting the girl.

At first Baxter didn't think she recognised Dee, because her reaction seemed curiously like dread. But then perhaps that was down to the short hair, ripped jeans and Doc Martens. They were scarcely Home Counties chic.

Dee, of course, knew her mother had recognised her the first instant. She counted the seconds that it took for her mother to recover and put on the semblance of delight that followed.

'Deborah…darling,' she cried, and came out on the terrace to greet her.

'Hello, Mother.' She met her halfway and suffered the obligatory embrace.

'Thank God you're all right,' her mother continued on a high note. 'I was so worried.'

'Were you?' Dee echoed, unwilling to play to the gallery.

That was what her mother was doing. For Baxter Ross, out from behind the driver's seat but keeping his distance as he leaned against the car roof.

'Of course. You're my daughter.' Her mother's eyes brimmed briefly with some emotion, but not long enough for Dee to identify it. 'Come along inside, darling…your friend, too,' she gushed on, her slightly puzzled glance including this male stranger.

Dee looked at him too, and wished she hadn't when he left his side of the car to approach them.

'This is Baxter, Mother—Mother, Baxter,' she introduced flatly.

'Pleased to meet you.' Baxter offered his hand, and the woman took it with a charming smile.

Dee watched her mother instantly warm to Baxter Ross and saw him through her mother's eyes: tall, handsome, well-mannered, and ultimately respectable in cream trousers and button-down shirt.

Dee gave a limited explanation of his presence. 'Baxter drove me up from London.'

'That was kind of you,' her mother applauded, then asked, 'Will you stay for tea?'

'He's in a hurry.' Dee's tone told him he wasn't welcome.

Baxter disregarded it, saying, 'I have time for tea.'

'Good.' Her mother looked pleased.

Dee understood only too well. Anything was better than the two of them being alone together.

When her mother turned to lead the way inside, Dee caught at Baxter's sleeve. 'You don't want to get involved in this.'

Baxter agreed, he didn't. But it niggled at him. Why would a girl run away from this comfortable home to live the life Dee had been leading in London?

'Your mother's waiting for us.' He shrugged off Dee's hand and picked up her bags to carry them inside for her.

He placed them at the foot of the stairs in the hall, and, ignoring another glare from the girl, waited for her to show him the way.

Dee followed her mother through to the kitchen.

It was then her mother observed, 'You've hurt your leg again. How did you do that?'

'I can't remember.' Dee didn't want to discuss her injuries with her mother. She watched her filling the kettle and asked, 'Where's Hetty?'

'It's her day off.' Her mother explained the house-keeper's absence.

'That's a shame. I'd have liked to see her.' Dee spoke without thinking.

Hetty came daily, and it took a moment or two for her mother to pick up the slip. She turned from rattling cups on saucers.

'You're not planning to stay?' She tried to sound disappointed.

But Dee knew. She saw it on her mother's face. Relief. Maybe things weren't so bad. Maybe Dee was just passing through.

'Dunno.' Dee was deliberately ungracious. 'I'm keeping my options open.'

'Oh.' Her mother looked doubtful, as if she didn't quite believe in these options.

And Dee found herself rattling on, 'Actually, Baxter has asked me to marry him and go live in his castle in Scotland. Romantic, isn't it?'

It was a wild claim, unlikely to go uncontested, but it was good—for a moment—to watch her mother's discon-certment.

Baxter Ross raised a questioning brow, too, as though asking what game she was playing, but otherwise seemed in no hurry to contradict her.

It was her mother who eventually said, 'Is this true? You and my daughter are planning to marry?'

Oddly he didn't deny it outright. 'It has been discussed, yes.'

Dee, who hadn't expected any support, stared at him in surprise.

'Well.' Her mother didn't hide her amazement. 'I don't know what to say.'

'You could try congratulations,' Dee suggested wick-edly.

'Yes, well…' Her mother was struggling with the cred-ibility gap. Dee might be her daughter but she still couldn't imagine a respectable-looking character like Baxter Ross falling for a wild child like her. 'I'm sorry, Mr—?'

'Ross—' Baxter supplied.

'But you're going to have to give me a chance to take this all in,' she ran on faintly. 'I mean…I don't know anything about you, and—'

'He's a doctor,' Dee supplied. 'That puts him above suspicion, doesn't it, Mother? Not likely to be—well, what shall we pick?—a crook, an opportunist, a child molester, maybe?'

Dee appeared to be talking off the top of her head, but her mother knew she wasn't.

'Dee.' Her distress was manifest in the way she was fingering the fine white pearls at her neck. 'Please. You can't come back and start this again.'

'Start?' Dee echoed. 'Start what, Mother?'

Dee had no intention of going further, not with a third party present. But her mother wasn't to know this.

'I'm sorry.' Her mother shook her head and backed towards the door. 'I'm going to have to ring Edward. You know I can't cope with this.'

Dee pulled a face as her mother flitted away—she was a social butterfly, without the courage to be anything else.

'Like to fill me in before she gets back?' Baxter Ross drawled.

'No,' Dee replied. 'Let's just get out of here before the cavalry arrives. I'll get Henry.'

She unlocked a set of French doors and walked onto the back terrace.

Baxter followed in disbelief. Did she really mean to leave without saying goodbye?

It seemed she had no conscience. He thought he might do well to remember that.

'You're not just going, are you?' He grabbed her arm and brought her to a halt.

'You've got the idea,' Dee threw back at him.

'You can't—not like this.' He pulled her back when she would have walked away.

'You don't know—' she began to protest.

'No, you're right, I don't know what wrong—imaginary

or otherwise—she's done to you,' he talked over her, 'but she's your mother. Surely she deserves better?'

'You don't get it, do you?' Dee rounded on him. 'You take one look at my mother and right away you're on her side. You think, How could that lovely woman produce a child like Dee? But if you knew the truth…'

'Tell me, then,' he demanded.

'And you'll believe it?' she countered.

Baxter hesitated. It was his downfall.

'I thought not,' she sneered in reply. 'Now, let go of me.'

She tried to twist from his grip. Baxter held onto her, assuming she would stop struggling. She didn't, and he finally released her.

She made a point of rubbing the red marks, before asking, 'Will you take Henry and me back to London?'

'No.'

'The nearest railway station, then?'

'No, not until you resolve things here,' he told her.

'Resolve things?' she echoed scornfully. 'You sound like a bloody therapist. Well, thanks, but I've already worked through my anger, grief, and any other repressed feelings you'd like to name…*Henry!*' she shouted at the dog. It was pointless, as he was deaf, but it was a good release for temper.

Baxter shadowed her down the steps to the garden where the dog had taken up residence in his kennel. She patted her leg, a command to come, but the retriever didn't move. He looked what he was—tired and old.

Baxter saw her face fall, as if her last friend in the world had deserted her.

'Deborah?' Her mother called out from the terrace above.

Gone was the chance of a clean getaway.

Baxter heard the note of anxiety in the older woman's voice, and said, 'Stay an hour, and then I'll give you a lift.'

Dee's eyes narrowed, as though testing if he meant it.

He checked his watch. 'We'll drink tea, make polite conversation and, if you still want to go, drive back at four o'clock.'

Back to what? A shop doorway? Dee felt a sudden loss

of nerve. Now she was back, wouldn't she be better staying?

She thought of her last time at home and quickly recovered her nerve. Better the devils she didn't know.

'Four o'clock.' She gave a nod of agreement.

'So, do we continue the pretence of an engagement?' he added.

'If that's okay?' Dee needed to impress her mother. 'Though I suppose we're not the most convincing of couples.'

'We could try being more so,' he suggested, and, putting an arm to her waist, began to gaze down at her.

'What are you doing?' she squeaked in surprise.

'Putting on a performance.' He nodded in the direction of the house, where her mother watched from the doorway. 'I could kiss you.'

'*Would* you?' Dee was even more surprised by this offer. He shrugged. 'If you like.'

'I…no…' Dee wasn't sure *she* wanted to do this.

But he was already doing it. His head blocked out the sun and his mouth moved over hers in a slow, unhurried kiss that had Dee catching her breath with the sheer, alarming sensuality of it. Without meaning to, she parted her lips and he deepened the kiss until she gave a moan, somewhere between pleasure and panic.

That she could feel desire for any man came as a shock to Dee, and, rather late, she began to pull away.

Baxter lifted his head from hers, in time to read her changing expression. 'You don't have to look quite so horrified just because you responded to me.'

'I didn't!' Even as Dee said it her body said something else, trembling against his lean, hard frame.

'Really?' He raised a brow. 'In that case, I can't wait until you *do* respond.'

His eyes lingered on her soft, bruised mouth as if he wanted to kiss her again.

Dee shook her head, denying that she felt anything, but made no effort to free herself.

She was caught between relief and annoyance when her mother called once more. 'Deborah, tea is ready.'

'Yes, Mother,' she called back, but didn't take her eyes off him.

'Yes, mother,' he mocked gently. 'We're very dutiful all of a sudden... Never mind, I think we were fairly convincing, don't you?'

He smiled in satisfaction, and Dee was left feeling used. Surely absurd, because she was using him, wasn't she?

'Well, it was no big deal from where I was standing,' she retaliated, 'but I guess it might fool someone at a distance.'

Dee was trying to sound blasé rather than insulting.

Whichever way he took it, the smile remained. Because he knew, of course. Knew just how convincing he'd been.

'Perhaps we should try a rerun,' he suggested, and started to draw her closer once more.

For a moment Dee had the strongest desire to go with it, shut her eyes and let his lips cover hers, feel again that rush of sensation as he held her in his arms.

But then her mother called once more and the moment was lost, and she broke away. The sound of quiet laughter followed her, telling her it had just been a game... For him, at least.

CHAPTER SIX

WHEN Dee arrived back at the house, her mother led the way through to the drawing room where she'd laid out afternoon tea.

'I telephoned Edward,' her mother informed her as they sat down. 'He's going to try and get away.'

'Do you seriously think I want to see him after the last time?' Dee's tone was one of disbelief. 'Or do you still imagine I'm trying to seduce your husband, Mother?'

Her mother looked pained, and, without meeting Dee's eyes, admitted, 'That was a misunderstanding. Edward explained it all later, after you'd gone...'

'I bet.' Dee had heard her stepfather's explanations.

'No, he was quite honest,' her mother ran on. 'He said it was entirely his fault. He hadn't meant to kiss you like that. It just happened. And I suppose, being young and curious, it was perfectly natural for you to respond—'

'I didn't!' It was an echo of the conversation she'd just had with Baxter Ross, only this time Dee had no doubts. She could still remember how she'd felt when her stepfather had kissed her—sick to the stomach.

'Darling,' her mother said, a slight whine in her voice, 'I'm not accusing you of anything, really I'm not. Clearly Edward got carried away. But if I can forgive a moment's madness...'

Then surely Dee could? Dee gazed at her mother. Did she really believe all this? Was she so stupid? Or just too frightened to believe anything else?

Barbara Litton fingered the pearls at her neck and still wouldn't look at Dee.

It was a betrayal of nerves, but it was also symbolic, that touching of jewels Edward's money had supplied. If she accepted Dee's version, then how could she go on living

with Edward? And without Edward, how could she survive?

'Anyway, darling—' the forced brightness returned to
her voice '—we don't need to speak of it again. Edward's
very sorry, and I'm sure he'll try his best to make it up to
you—'

'We can't stay longer than an hour,' Dee cut across her
mother's fantasies and lied without conscience. 'We're on
our way to Baxter's family in Scotland.'

'They know about you and him?' her mother queried.

'Yes, and they're quite delighted,' Dee claimed extravagantly. 'They were beginning to think he'd never find the
right woman.'

'They've met you?'

'Not yet.'

'Oh.' Barbara studied Dee a moment before saying ten-
tatively, 'Do you think…? Well, it's just a bit of advice,
darling…that you might want to dress a little more femininely?'

'To gain their approval, you mean?'

'Yes.'

Her mother looked hopeful.

'Then, no,' Dee responded, 'I don't want to dress more
femininely. You see, I no longer care if people approve of
me, Mother. I guess that's what begging does for you.'

'You've been begging?' Barbara Litton was appalled.

'It was either that or turn tricks for middle-aged punters
in business suits,' Dee stated bluntly. 'And I could have
stayed at home to do that.'

'Deborah!' her mother reproved in shock.

Dee turned cold eyes on her. 'What?'

It was a challenge. Let her mother face the truth for once.

But, of course, that wasn't her mother's way.

'I don't understand what's happened to you,' Barbara
Litton said in distraught tones. 'You were such a sweet
child. You had every advantage, everything you ever
wanted. Why do you have to—?' she broke off as she noticed Baxter Ross in the doorway.

Dee wasn't similarly inhibited. 'Why do I have to do
what, Mother?'

But her mother ignored her and fixed back on her polite hostess smile. 'Please come and have some tea.'

Baxter nodded and, passing a vacant armchair, came to sit with Dee on the sofa. Perhaps he intended playing the devoted fiancé.

Dee, however, slumped inelegantly back on her mother's cream watersilk sofa and took a cigarette out.

'I wish you wouldn't,' her mother appealed quietly. When Dee ignored her and lit up, she added with a sigh, 'I'll fetch an ashtray.'

When she was gone, Baxter asked, 'Why can't you at least be civil to her?'

It was too much for Dee. 'You be civil to her if you like her that much,' she suggested, rising to her feet. 'I'm going to fetch some things.'

She limped off, leaving him to it. She knew her mother wouldn't reveal anything important in her absence.

She went upstairs to her room. It was light and airy, with anything a teenaged girl could want, but she felt no desire to stay. She started rifling through drawers and the wardrobe for clothing that would be practical on the street. Much of it was dresses, and trendy tops and skirts that could only be worn indoors.

She selected jeans and a ribbed T-shirt and changed into them, discarding her torn clothes on the floor. She was shocked to discover how loose they were at the waist, although oddly her breasts hadn't shrunk. She found a wide belt and tied it to the last hole to make the jeans fit.

She packed another set of trousers and a T-shirt in a duffle bag and looked unsuccessfully for a jacket before settling for a long wool jumper which might offer some warmth at night. Then, fairly certain it was the last time she would be home, she started to sort through a shoe box where she kept her personal possessions.

Mostly it contained certificates, photographs and mementoes from past holidays and happier times. She went through it systematically, tearing up much of it, taking out a couple of photographs of her father. She was saying a final goodbye to her childhood, and she knew it.

She wasn't aware of time passing until the door opened

behind her. She stood and turned, expecting to see Baxter. Then she froze.

Dressed in his expensive Savile Row suit was Edward Litton—the epitome of a successful surgeon. Suave, handsome and as cultured as they came. Once Dee would have trusted him with her life.

'Deborah.' He smiled in greeting. 'It's so good to see you.'

He took a step towards her, arms outstretched. Dee violently recoiled.

'Touch me and I'll kill you,' she said.

The smile faded, but his manner remained smooth. 'Don't be so dramatic, darling. I'm not going to hurt you. I'd never hurt you. You know that.'

'Stop it.' Dee couldn't stomach listening to this once more.

He frowned, as if he had no idea what she meant. 'I'm so glad you're home,' he continued, as if she hadn't spoken. 'We've been out of our minds with worry. You hear such stories of the things that happen to young girls in London… That is where you've been?'

Dee nodded rather than speak. She couldn't believe his concerned tones. Didn't he remember the last time they'd seen each other?

'Well, you can tell us about it in your own time,' he said, as if she'd merely been on holiday. 'The important thing is that you've returned. We've really missed you.'

He caught and held her eyes for a moment and Dee realised it was true. He, at least, *had* missed her. It was an irony, when her own mother clearly hadn't.

'What have you done to your hair?' His tone was indulgent, though he probably hated it.

'I couldn't keep it clean so I had it cut,' Dee replied shortly.

'You look thinner, too.' His eyes travelled over her body.

Baxter Ross had made a similar comment, but it wasn't the same thing. He hadn't made her flesh creep.

'Nothing a few good meals won't put right.' He smiled once more.

'I'm not staying,' she said.

'We'll see,' he replied, as if he didn't believe her. After all, she'd been persuaded to stay the last time.

'No, we won't see.' Her voice hardened and she crossed to the door, forgetting her packed bag.

Edward took warning from her expression and stepped out of her way, but he trailed after her along the landing. 'Come on, Deborah, listen to me just for a moment...'

'No, you listen to me!' Dee rounded on him furiously. 'This isn't stupid, trusting little Deborah any more. You destroyed her, remember?'

He looked sad rather than angry. Why did she have to say these things?

'Aren't you being a little harsh...? I admit I behaved impetuously.' He gave her a rueful look. 'But your mother's forgiven me so why can't you?'

Dee shook her head in disbelief. Was she the only person in this house with a grasp of reality?

'Edward, I'm your stepdaughter and you tried to...to rape me!' She forced out the words so there would be no going back. No pretending everything was sunshine and light. No kidding herself or him that they could live in the same house.

She watched the colour—of rage or shame?—seep into Edward's face. She made to walk away, but he caught her arm. 'Deborah—'

He was going to plead with her, but he didn't get the chance.

'Dee!' Baxter called from downstairs.

'Up here,' she called back in relief.

'Who's that?' Edward asked quickly.

Dee almost relished saying, 'My fiancé.'

'What?' His shock was evident. 'He can't be.'

Dee knew what he meant. The man climbing the stairs had an air of maturity and confidence that made an infatuation with a seventeen-year-old schoolgirl seem highly unlikely.

'Think he's too old, do you?' The irony in her voice couldn't be missed.

Baxter arrived at the top of the stairs, aware of the other man's scrutiny. 'Aren't you going to introduce us?'

'No,' Dee said with uncompromising rudeness.

He was left to introduce himself. 'Baxter Ross... You must be Dee's stepfather.'

'Yes, Edward Litton.' Edward briefly took the hand offered to him. 'I'm afraid you have the advantage on me, Mr Ross.'

It was Dee who corrected, '*Dr* Ross.'

Baxter slid her a questioning look.

'You're a GP,' Edward concluded, in his I'm-a-senior-consultant manner.

'Actually, no, he's something terribly important in the Red Cross in Africa,' Dee invented liberally. 'Or at least he was. He's about to switch to a top research post in tropical medicine.'

Baxter raised a brow in Dee's direction, but she didn't care.

'Impressive,' Edward commented briefly. 'I prefer hands-on medicine myself. Much more rewarding.'

'I'll say,' Dee agreed deceptively. 'How much is it these days for varicose veins? A couple of grand?'

Edward's face constricted before he forced a laugh. 'I'm afraid Deborah can have quite a sharp sense of humour.'

'So I've discovered,' Baxter concurred.

'Though you can't always take too seriously what she says,' Edward qualified.

Dee saw immediately what he was doing—covering his back, should she have confessed all.

This time Baxter Ross remained silent, his eyes narrowed slightly in her stepfather's direction. Dee wondered what he was thinking.

Edward dropped his confiding air as he went on to say, 'For instance, she's just told me the two of you are engaged. I assume that's a joke.'

Baxter's eyes switched back to Dee. Her face was mute with appeal.

'Really, why do you assume that?' His answer gave little away.

'Well, naturally...you are aware Deborah's only seventeen?' Edward took the moral high ground.

The hypocrisy of it left Dee speechless.

Baxter Ross didn't bat an eyelid. 'Is that significant?'

'In law it certainly is,' Edward blustered. 'You need parental permission to marry anyone under the age of eighteen.'

'So what?' Dee shrugged. 'Mum will give it. She'd let me marry Jack the Ripper if it meant an easy life.'

'Your mother will do what I advise,' Edward claimed with some confidence. 'And, no offence to you, Dr Ross, but we'd have to know you much better before we could contemplate a man so much older marrying our daughter. I'm sure you understand.'

Baxter nodded. 'I'm beginning to.'

'Good.' Dee's stepfather thought he'd won this round.

Dee wasn't so sure. She'd learned not to underestimate Baxter Ross.

'So why don't we go down to my study and discuss this matter?' Edward suggested in almost cordial tones. 'There could be things, after all, that you'd like to know about us or Deborah,' he added with a smile.

Baxter smiled back, and Dee's heart dropped. Five minutes of Edward playing concerned stepfather with troubled daughter and Baxter would be in his car and away.

But, no, Baxter Ross seemed to be playing his own game as he glanced at his watch and said, 'I'm afraid we're running late. Some other time, maybe... Dee, are you ready?'

Dee stared at him in disbelief for a moment, then curbed an impulse to hug him. 'I've collected some stuff in the bedroom I'd like to take.'

'I'll get it.' He walked past Edward, treating him like furniture, and went into the room Dee indicated.

Edward looked apoplectic. 'Who does he think he is?'

'Sir Galahad.' Dee felt a little high and frivolous. 'And, if I were you, I wouldn't get in his way.'

Edward took this as a physical threat, which Dee had fairly much intended, and, with an impotent look of anger, he hurried downstairs.

'What was all that about?' Baxter asked when he rejoined her on the landing.

'Nothing!' Dee snapped rather too fiercely.

He raised a brow, but let it go for now, and fell in by her side as she began limping back down to the hall.

They were at the front door when Edward reappeared with her mother in tow.

'Tell her, Barbara,' Edward commanded. 'Tell her she can't possibly disappear again, especially with some man old enough to be her father.'

All eyes turned to Barbara Litton. She was visibly nervous.

'Darling, Edward says if you come back everything will be fine,' she finally relayed.

Dee didn't know whether to despise or pity her mother.

'You don't really believe that, do you, Mother?' She caught and held her mother's eyes, and willed her to face up to the truth.

'I—I...'

'Barbara!'

Her stepfather's hectoring tone was insistent, but, for once, it had the opposite effect.

Slowly her mother shook her head from side to side, and, having found courage from somewhere, appealed to Baxter, 'You will look after her, won't you?'

Dee glanced sideways in time to see Baxter nod his head with a gravity that could almost have been real.

It certainly deceived her mother, because the briefest smile crossed her face before she drifted off—both mentally and physically—towards the living room.

Edward cursed under his breath.

Dee ignored him, picking up the flute case and rucksack she'd left earlier. Baxter took the rucksack from her, shouldered it and held the extra bag in one hand while he put the other to her elbow and led her outside.

Reaction was setting in, and Dee felt shaky on both legs. She leaned against the side of the car and waited until he stowed away her bags before asking, 'Will you fetch Henry for me?'

Baxter glanced towards her stepfather, who was now standing in the doorway. 'You'll be all right?'

Dee nodded, and he left her to walk round the side of the house, ignoring Edward.

Edward saw his chance and approached. Dee stood her ground rather than scuttle into the car. She had suddenly stopped fearing this man.

'Deborah, please,' he appealed to her once more. 'You can't go like this. What do you know of this man?'

Very little, Dee could have admitted, but said instead, 'I know he isn't going to attack me when he's drunk!'

Her stepfather flinched. 'I suppose I deserved that. But if you could just understand how it is, living with your mother. I thought she was so serene, so beautiful when I married her, but there's so little substance to her. She hasn't half your intelligence or your courage, your passion... Is it any wonder that I feel the way I do about you?'

He reached a hand up to touch her face, a gesture of seemingly genuine tenderness.

Still Dee recoiled from him. 'Don't!'

'I can't help it.' He caught her arm when she would have walked away. 'Little Deborah... I stayed for you, you know.'

His gaze told her he was serious, but all Dee felt was anger. If he loved her—really loved her—he wouldn't be playing on her emotions like this.

She twisted from his grip. 'Leave me alone, Edward, or I'll call for Baxter,' she threatened.

It worked, especially as they both glanced round to find that Baxter was already standing at the corner of the house, restraining Henry, while he watched the tense scene between the two.

He approached, his face tight with anger, and Edward went into rapid retreat to the house.

Baxter threw a dismissive glance at the other man before ordering, 'Get in!'

Dee didn't argue. She wanted to get away, too. She just wondered what Baxter had overheard.

He slammed the boot door on Henry, then climbed behind the driver's wheel, turned on the engine and accelerated rapidly.

At length Dee muttered, 'I don't know why you're mad with me. I told you not to get involved.'

'That was all you told me,' he responded, his tone clipped and harsh.

Any gratitude Dee might have felt went out of the window. 'So what did you expect?'

His mouth thinned even more. 'Some indication of what was going on between you and Litton might have been useful.'

'Going on?' Her voice rose with her temper. 'What do you mean?'

Baxter found his own temper rising. He was tired of this girl taking him for a fool. He spotted a layby ahead and pulled off the road.

He confronted her. 'What do you think I mean...*little Deborah?*'

Dee's eyes flashed with anger. 'Don't call me that!'

'Then stop playing games,' he threw back. 'I may not have heard it all, but I certainly got the gist from his body language!'

And the wrong idea, Dee realised, if he imagined she'd welcomed it.

She could have protested, could have tried to explain, but what was the point? He wasn't going to believe her. She came from a nice middle-class home with nice middle-class manners, and no one was ever going to believe her.

He took her silence for guilt, and wounded her further with, 'No wonder your mother wanted you gone.'

That was no more than the truth, but it hurt; oh, how it hurt.

'You don't understand,' she said, a catch in her voice.

'Then explain it!' he bit back.

But Dee didn't have the heart for it any more.

The reality of her situation suddenly overwhelmed her. Her mother had closed the door. She was nobody's daughter any more. She was finally, irretrievably homeless.

Baxter watched in disbelief as the first tear slipped down her face.

'God, you're not going to cry on me!'

'No!' Dee denied, even as a second tear followed it.

She swallowed hard and turned her face to the window. She didn't want to cry in front of this man.

He sighed loudly. 'Look, forget it. You don't have to explain anything. It's none of my business.'

Dee was too choked to answer. She shook her head. She wanted to be left alone.

Baxter realised then that he was incidental. These tears weren't for him.

Still angry, he tried to remain immune. Her back was to him, but he saw her shoulders heave, heard the first sob, listened to the despair in the next.

Soon she was crying like a child, and it was too much for him. He released both their seat belts and reached to comfort her.

She resisted, pushing at his shoulders, sobbing, 'You understand nothing, nothing, nothing...' She was angry with him, angry with the world.

She balled her fists into his chest but he went on holding her, urging softly, 'Tell me, then. Tell me.' He was ready to accept her grief and pain.

Dee shook her head even as she stopped struggling to be free, and began to rock like a baby in his arms, crying out in anguish, 'I have nobody!'

No words could answer such desperation so Baxter just gathered her closer, with a hand to the back of her head, stilling it against his shoulder, while he murmured against her hair—soothing noises he would have made to a young niece.

She continued to cry, but the sobs diminished until only silent tears slid from her eyes.

Dee felt him stroking her hair, and it was comforting at first, but then her emotions seemed to shift and she trembled in awareness of him. It wasn't fear exactly, but she stirred in his arms, conscious once more of the fact he was a man.

He let her draw away but held her at arm's length. She felt his eyes on her face, and was embarrassed to realise she was still crying.

'Have you a handkerchief?' he asked her quietly.

She raised her eyes to his and shook her head. 'I'll stop in a moment,' she promised, feeling foolish.

'It doesn't matter,' he told her softly, one hand lifting to tilt her head up while he used the other to wipe away her tears.

She stared at him, transfixed, while long, tapering fingers smoothed over her cheekbones. His gentleness was overwhelming, a revelation. Her tears dried, by some miracle, although the breath caught in her throat as he finally cradled her face with one hand.

'What are we going to do with you?' He spoke as if to a child, but it only added to Dee's confusion.

She didn't want to be a child to him. She wanted...

He leaned towards her, meaning to place a light kiss on her cheek, but she raised her head slightly and his mouth brushed hers by accident.

It was unintentional, but Baxter had no excuse for his next action other than the flicker of response he'd felt from her lips and her apparent willingness to be kissed like this.

All he remembered was that one moment he'd been thinking of her as a kid and the next she was a soft, warm woman in his arms, kissing him back so sweetly the blood raced through his veins.

It was over almost before it began as sanity returned and he broke away, breathing hard.

He swore at himself, not her, then caught her stricken look. 'I'm sorry. It's no answer. I shouldn't have touched you.'

But he had. He had touched her with his gentleness, slipping past her guard for a heartbeat or two. She had laid herself open to being hurt, so why be surprised when it happened?

He said something else; Dee didn't bother listening. She curled away from him and turned her face to the window. She had an idea that she'd made a fool of herself, but was suddenly too tired to care.

When he asked simply, 'Scotland or London?' she answered with a shrug. Neither place meant anything to her. No place did any more.

The decision was left to Baxter. He wished he hadn't kissed her. It made him feel guilty even as it reinforced his growing belief that taking her to Scotland was a recipe for disaster.

He had to harden his heart and remind himself that he was no longer in the business of saving the world. Two years of war had earned him the right to some peace, and nothing about this girl promised that.

Why was he even debating it? He had walked away from the dead and dying. He could surely walk away from one girl.

He started the car and headed for London.

CHAPTER SEVEN

'ARE we here?' Dee asked at the end of their journey.

He nodded. 'Finally, yes.'

She rubbed sleep from her eyes and peered out. There was no moon, no street lights, no houses, just darkness. They were sitting at the end of a dirt track in the middle of nowhere, facing some ruined tower.

Dee felt a twinge of alarm. 'I thought you said you lived in Edinburgh.'

'Outside Edinburgh,' he corrected.

She looked round for some sign of habitation. 'Where, exactly?'

'There, exactly.' He nodded towards the lump of stone in front of them.

'You're kidding.' She laughed. He didn't laugh back. 'In that…*thing?*'

She couldn't think of another word for it.

'You know what they say,' he responded. 'Be careful of what you wish for and all that.'

'Come again?' This ruin had never been on Dee's wish list.

'You told your mother I had a castle in Scotland,' he reminded her.

'Yeah,' she conceded. 'Well, I was thinking more in the line of Balmoral… Is this really yours?'

Dee still wasn't sure if it was some kind of joke. In fact, the whole journey had had an unreal air. She remembered crying, of course, after they'd left Oakfield, and him holding her until her tears had dried. She remembered his tenderness and the surprise of it, and the feelings it had stirred in her, so that when they had kissed, almost by accident, she had not pushed him away. She'd tried to forget the rest, but it kept coming back to her—the way she'd felt as his lips moved over hers, the sweet, painful urge to respond.

That was the most unreal thing of all, yet it remained the most vivid.

Everything after that had passed in a dream. She'd stared out of the window, vaguely aware of signs stating miles to London, exhausted into a blessed emotional numbness before sleep actually began to overtake her. She hadn't fought it, knowing she might later have to spend the night awake in a doorway, too scared to shut her eyes.

She didn't know how long she'd slept but when she'd woken it was to find the signs were now recording places like Sheffield and Barnsley, and she'd realised they were many miles from London.

'I'm taking you home for a while,' was all Baxter had said.

It was all he'd needed to say for Dee to go along with it. One place seemed the same as another now that she was rootless.

They had stopped at a couple of motorway service stations *en route*. He had eaten and drunk coffee. She had smoked and ignored his disapproval. They had made no plans past getting up here.

'Here' being this godforsaken spot in a dark, desolate landscape that could have stepped out of the pages of a Robert Louis Stevenson novel—only it was all too real as he confirmed dryly, 'Yes, it really is mine.'

She pulled a face in vague apology as she realised she was insulting his home, which presumably he loved, gloom and doom notwithstanding.

'It's more habitable than it looks,' he assured her, stepping out of the car.

Dee sincerely hoped it was.

She tried to get out her side, but her knee had stiffened once more. He came round and helped her out, keeping a guiding hand at her elbow. They picked their way over rough grass, then through a gate in a low wall, before a floodlight suddenly came on, illuminating the ground surrounding the tower.

Dee looked up and saw a series of small windows cut into the black stone. They were recent additions to a building that must be several centuries old. She counted four,

6

maybe five floors. Even lit, it looked a cold, inhospitable place.

They skirted the tower until they reached a stout oak door. He rang the bell rather than open it.

Dee frowned. 'You don't live on your own, then?'

'Usually I do,' he stated. 'At the moment someone is caretaking it for me.'

Someone? She gave him a quizzical look, but it was ignored. Her heart sank a little as she wondered whether it would be a female someone.

'Haven't you a key?' she asked, when he kept ringing the bell and getting no response.

'Naturally,' he responded. 'But as it's two in the morning I don't want to creep in unannounced. Joseph might take us for burglars.'

'It's a man!' Dee concluded in relief, and drew an odd look for it.

'More a boy. Joseph's only eighteen,' he explained. Then, in case she might still be harbouring any wrong ideas, went on 'He's the son of a friend, nothing more. You understand?'

Dee nodded. He hadn't needed to say anything. She no longer doubted his sexuality.

'Is he expecting us?'

'He knows I'm due home this week.'

But not her, Dee concluded.

'He doesn't appear to be home.' His expression reflected mild surprise. 'Stay here.'

He left her to do a quick tour round the outside of the tower. Dee wasn't sure what he was looking for. She just wished he would come back soon. The floodlights had gone off and they were back to being in pitch dark. Henry was growling low in his throat, even though he couldn't hear the rustlings and snufflings and night noises that were making her decidedly jumpy.

'Baxter?' she eventually called out, losing her nerve.

He didn't call back, and she shouted louder. Still there was no response, but the floodlights came on once more. Then another minute or two ticked by before she heard approaching footsteps.

Common sense said it had to be Baxter, but she ducked out of sight behind a thick wooden beam shoring up part of the wall.

'Dee, where are you?' he demanded, finding her gone.

She emerged from her hiding place, and demanded in return, 'Where have you been?'

He raised a quizzical brow at her tone, but answered all the same. 'Checking the generator shed to see if Joseph's moped was there. It isn't, so I think we'll let ourselves in.'

He used his key and she followed him inside, finding herself at the base of a spiral stone staircase.

'You go first,' he suggested. 'It's two flights up, so take your time.'

Dee gave him no argument. With her injured knee, she could do little else.

She caught her breath on the first landing, while he indicated the two doors leading off it.

'That's the main hall. I use it as a living area. The other door is the kitchen.'

He didn't open either, but Dee imagined the kitchen would be something out of another century.

They continued up the spiral staircase, and he explained that the second and third floors housed bedrooms and a study. On the second landing there were again two doors leading off.

'You have this one.' He pushed open the heavy door on his right and switched on a light, before backing out again. 'I'm going to check whether Joseph's home or not.'

He crossed the landing to knock quietly on the other door, and left Dee to go into her room by herself. She'd expected fairly basic accommodation, and stood stock-still in the doorway as she discovered a bedroom literally fit for a king, albeit one from a different age.

The walls were stone, hung with landscape canvases, and the ceilings were high. A polished oak floor was scattered with rich woollen rugs, and a recess contained an open fireplace. The furniture was mostly dark, heavy pieces, dominated by an immense four-poster bed at the far wall.

She limped towards it and sat on the brocade counterpane, picking up a piece of paper from the pillow. She read it before she wondered whether she should.

Greetings, little brother,

The heating is on, the fridge is full and the cleaning firm has been. Joseph is staying with friends in Edinburgh. The question is—*where are you?* You'd better call the moment you arrive or suffer the consequences!

From the devoted sister you definitely don't deserve,

Cat.

Having read it once, Dee had no compunction about reading it a second time. It was such an unfamiliar perspective—Baxter Ross as someone's little brother. In fact, it took a leap of imagination to even believe he'd been a child.

She dropped the letter sharpish as he knocked on her door and called, 'Dee?'

'Yes?' she replied and, when he didn't appear, called back, 'Come in.'

He did so, but no further than the doorway. 'Is there anything you need?'

'No…well, a toothbrush would be nice.'

'Through that door—' he nodded to the back wall '—you'll find a bathroom. There's probably one there you could use.'

'Thanks….and, um, I don't suppose you have an old shirt?'

'What for?'

'A nightdress,' she explained. 'I haven't got one.'

He walked across to a wardrobe and took out the first shirt he came to. 'This do?'

'Yeah, fine.' Dee took it from his hand. It was crisp white and blue striped cotton. 'Are you sure? It looks fairly new.'

He gave an indifferent shrug. 'It's not the sort of thing I wear.'

She supposed it wasn't. He seemed to favour cream or

khaki trousers and button-down denim shirts. This was more businessman-style.

'My sister bought it for me,' he explained. 'So, as long as she doesn't see you in it, you're welcome to it.'

'Your sister buys your clothes?' she asked.

'Some of them,' he admitted. 'I usually don't have the time… Why, is that significant of something?' A smile said he really didn't care if it was.

'Probably,' Dee quipped back. 'But I'm not sure what.'

'Well, when you work it out, let my sister know,' he added dryly.

Dee understood from this that his sister did things for him whether he liked it or not. She remembered the letter.

'Actually, she's left you a note.' She handed it to him.

He scanned it quickly, smiling slightly, before folding it and putting it in his pocket.

'Right, I'll leave you to it,' he said. 'Unless you wish me to rebandage your leg?'

'No, thanks.' Dee trusted him well enough. She just wasn't comfortable with their doctor-patient relationship.

He shrugged, before walking towards the door. 'I'll be one floor up if you should need me.'

She nodded. 'This is your room, isn't it?'

'Normally, yes,' he confirmed.

Dee's face reflected a degree of guilt.

He misread her expression. 'Don't worry, I won't try to reclaim it—or anything else—in the dead of night.'

'That wasn't…I didn't think…' She trailed off, for once inarticulate.

He had no such problem. 'No, well, I wouldn't blame you if you had. Kissing you earlier—that was a mistake.'

'Yes,' she agreed, hoping he would leave it at that.

But he continued in rational tones, 'You were obviously at a low point and vulnerable, and I should have respected the fact… I can only say it's a while since I've held a woman, and I guess baser instincts took over.'

Dee's heart lifted briefly at the idea of him seeing her as a woman, before she analysed the rest. It pretty much added up to the fact that she'd been there and seemingly available.

'That wasn't intended as an insult,' he added, observing her darkening scowl. 'I'm just trying to—'

'Forget it,' Dee cut in, before he could embarrass them both further. And, motivated by pride, she claimed, 'It's hardly a big deal. I've kissed lots of men... Fortunately most of them don't agonise about it afterwards.'

She'd meant to sound blasé, but overachieved slightly. Still, the sudden rigidity in his jaw muscles had to be better than the look of pity it replaced.

'Okay, I'll try and remember that—assuming I ever want to join the crowd.' Contempt laced his voice as he delivered this parting shot.

By the time Dee could think of a suitable reply, he had already gone.

He left the door ajar, and she listened to his ascending footsteps on the stone staircase, cursing him and her own stupidity. She hadn't wanted him to think her pathetic, so now he considered her free-and-easy. Great!

She sank her weight onto the bed and, refusing to worry about it, sent a critical eye round his room instead. It was as austere as the man himself. Furnished in traditional woods, it had few feminine touches apart from a large spray of flowers and fern arranged in the fireplace. Was that his sister's doing?

They were obviously close—perhaps bonded tighter by the early death of their parents. It was a relationship Dee could only imagine. At one time she had longed for a brother or sister, but it appeared her mother had found Dee's birth too traumatic to repeat. Now she was all alone in the world.

She dashed at a tear, refusing to cry. She had to be strong. After all, where had being weak and dependent got her? Holed up in a ruined tower with Dr 'Superior' Ross.

Well, perhaps ruined was an exaggeration, she conceded as she wandered through to the adjoining bathroom and found it to be strictly late-twentieth-century modern, including bidet and power shower.

She found the toothbrush he'd mentioned, and brushed her teeth hard. As she did so she caught sight of herself in the mirror above the washhand basin and was shocked by the image. She knew what she'd used to look like; she'd been reminded that afternoon by a photograph of a smiling girl with long blonde hair, beautiful skin and a face that had flesh as well as cheekbones.

A stranger stared back at her now. The cropped hair had grown a little, but was dull and boy-short, the multiple earrings were merely disfiguring, while her face was so pale and hollowed that she could have been suffering some terminal illness. She wanted to cry again, this time for the loss of her looks.

She pulled out the earrings one by one, then looked again. She still didn't like herself. She realised it had been possibly weeks since she'd properly taken care of her hair. She reached up into a cabinet and found bottles of shampoo and conditioner. They smelt outdoorsy and masculine, but that hardly mattered.

She turned on the power shower, and a cascade of hot water drummed on the base of it. She stripped off and climbed in. She did her hair first, then simply leaned against the shower stall, letting the water wash over her. When her leg began to ache, she slid to a sitting position and drew her knees up to rest her head on them.

She lost all sense of time, or place, or anything but her unhappiness, as she sat and let the water drum over her in a vain attempt to wash her sorrow away.

Stripped down to boxer shorts, Baxter climbed into the spare bed, ready to sleep for a week. He didn't want to think of the girl and her blasted problems, or his sister's reaction to this new complication in his life. Tomorrow would be too soon for that.

He switched off the light and waited for sleep to overtake him. It almost did. He was just drifting off when a banging noise made him start awake.

For a split second he thought himself back in Africa, and tensed, ready for the next shot, then laughed at his panic as water gurgled through a pipe. It was only the girl running a tap.

He was waiting for the next bang, and groaned aloud

when it came. He had renovated the electrics and the fittings, but the plumbing had had to wait. There was miles of it yet to be mapped, thick, ancient pipes from another era that were prone to air locks and percussion effects.

He expected it to stop, but it didn't. She must be showering rather than washing. He shut his eyes and tried to sleep. Perhaps he might have if the banging had had a rhythm, but it was intermittent, and sometimes explosively loud.

In the ten years since his grandfather had ceded this tower to him, he had yet to find a permanent solution for the musical pipework. Normally it didn't matter. Normally he lived alone, and if anyone was running water in the dead of night it was himself.

He waited in the dark for the banging to cease, consulting the luminous dials of his watch from time to time. The minutes gradually mounted. It was now past three a.m. He cursed her again. Who took showers at such a time? Even if she needed to wash, couldn't she wait until it was light?

Seemingly, no, she couldn't; the water kept rushing through the pipes, banging each time it encountered an air lock. Baxter supposed it might be a reaction to living rough, a feeling that one might never get clean again. He glanced at his watch again and did a quick calculation. She'd now been showering for a total of thirty-four minutes.

He gave it another ten minutes before he got up and slipped back into his trousers. He didn't bother with a shirt or socks but, temper rising, went back down the spiral staircase. He knocked at her door loud enough to wake her if she'd somehow fallen asleep with the shower left on. When he drew no reply, he walked into the room and, seeing the bed empty, strode towards the bathroom door. He knocked hard on it, and kept knocking, not anxious to walk in on her. He didn't fancy a hysterical female on his hands.

'Dee! Dee!' He shouted her name several times, but still elicited no response. 'Answer if you can hear me, dammit!'

Nothing. He felt his patience snapping. The bathroom door was a modern panel one, and even with the shower on she must surely have heard him.

He tried the handle, not really expecting it to give, and

found himself in the bathroom, having not considered his next move.

Dee was oblivious. Her hearing had gone under the pressure of the water. She was still sitting down, head on her knees, when the shower stall was suddenly opened.

She lifted unfocused eyes to Baxter Ross and tried to get her brain round what he was doing there. Later, she wondered why she hadn't screamed. After all, she was naked and he only partly clothed. But at the time she just stared at him, and he at her, at the water streaming down her upturned face, and her stick-thin body, huddled and shivering despite the heat of the electric shower.

He was the first to move, reaching in to switch off the water and at the same time handing her an enormous bath towel to cover her nakedness.

'Here. Wrap this round you,' he instructed quietly, and when she made no move to do so did it for her.

He lost her in the folds of the towel, then half lifted her cramped body from the stall. He closed the toilet seat and perched her there, and, when he was sure she wasn't going to fall off, took a step back from her.

Dee's ears popped and she tried to concentrate on what he was saying, but lost interest in his description of the technicalities of air locks. She secured the towel sarong-style round her upper body, leaving her arms bare but the rest covered. Not that he showed the remotest interest in her state of undress.

'Do you know how long you've been in that shower?' he demanded.

Dee shook her head, and a shrug said she didn't care either.

'The skin on your feet is shrivelled,' he pointed out, 'and God only knows what harm you might have done your leg.'

Dee's mouth went into a conscious pout. She found she wasn't nervous of him, or particularly embarrassed. She just wished he would go away or stop giving her a hard time.

He did neither, crouching beside her instead and pushing the towel past her knee to reveal a soaked, unravelling bandage. He unwound the rest.

'Just look at it!' he said, on exposing the knee. 'Come on, look!'

Dee refused, tilting her head upwards as she retorted, 'No one's asking you to do anything about it... In fact, I want you to leave—this minute!'

He stretched to his full height again. Dee thought he was about to go, and suddenly the desperation returned.

She felt relief when he reached up to unlock a medicine cabinet and take down a fresh crêpe bandage. He wasn't leaving, but she didn't flatter herself over his motives for staying. It was just that he was a doctor, first and foremost.

She watched as he worked in tight-lipped silence, winding the bandage round and round her swollen knee, close but careful not to touch, as if touching her would be distasteful to him. It was hard now to believe how tenderly he had held her when she had cried that afternoon.

'If you don't start looking after this knee,' he told her gruffly, 'you could end up with a permanent injury.'

'Would you care?' Dee threw back.

He glanced up at her and raised a brow before commenting dryly, 'We are feeling sorry for ourselves.'

Dee glared back. 'If this is your bedside manner, I'd definitely stick to dead people.'

He understood the insult, but laughed all the same. 'Why do you think I'm going into research?'

He didn't like people. Was that what he meant?

'There.' He finished the bandage with a safety pin and, standing, put an arm to her waist. 'Right, hold on.'

He lifted her and she was left to grab onto his shoulders.

'I can walk!' She tried to wriggle out of his arms.

He held her fast, warning, 'You're dislodging your towel.'

She followed his gaze to find one breast exposed. She tried to cover it but only succeeded in losing more of her towel as he carried her through.

She told herself it didn't matter. He wouldn't be interested.

But she was wrong. His eyes remained on her body as he laid her down on his four-poster bed. She rapidly covered herself.

Caught staring, he didn't pretend he'd been doing otherwise.

'Sorry, it was the surprise.'

'What?'

'You have breasts.' He stated the obvious.

Dee was stung into stating the obvious back. 'I *am* a
girl!'

'Well-developed breasts,' he qualified, with a slight
smile.

This time Dee didn't know how to react. It was a surprise
to her as well—while her arms and legs grew thinner, her
breasts had remained full. But somehow she didn't think
they were just discussing biology here.

Baxter saw a look of nervousness cross her face, and
continued in a drawl, 'Don't worry. I still wasn't planning
a grand seduction scene. Here.'

He handed her his striped shirt, then very pointedly stood
with his back to her while she sat up and dressed. It seemed
he had no wish to see the rest of her naked.

'I know that!' Dee claimed when he eventually turned
round again, and, in reckless mood, added, 'Perhaps women
really *aren't* your thing.'

She said it as a half-jibe, half-joke. She didn't expect
him to take it seriously.

But Baxter did, and found he minded now; his voice
hardened as he responded, 'I thought we'd sorted that out.
I am not homosexual. That was a complete misconcep-
tion…yours!'

Dee knew that too, but wasn't about to admit it. He was
normally so cool it was enjoyable to see him riled.

There was a trace of a smile on her lips when she eventually answered, 'If you say so.'

'I do!' The words were ground out between clenched
teeth.

Perhaps she should have taken warning at that point, instead of smirking, 'Fine.'

'You don't believe me, do you?' he challenged, pro-
voked to anger by her baiting. 'Or maybe you just want me
to prove it… Is that it?'

Dee didn't understand what the latter meant until it was

too late. One moment he was standing over her, the next he was beside her on the bed, his hand on one of her arms, keeping her there.

In the first instant Dee froze, then he caught her other arm and brought her round to face him. She fought down panic, but still betrayed herself in the fine trembling of her body.

His brows drew together, questioning her reaction. 'You're not scared of me?'

He said it in disbelief, but then he imagined her to be brave to the point of foolishness. Mostly she was. It was just the man-woman thing that gave her problems.

'No,' she lied.

'You don't have to be. I would never do anything you didn't want,' he added in softer tones.

'No,' she repeated, unable to find another word.

Because she *was* scared. Not the way she had been with her stepfather—this time it was her emotions over which she had no control.

She just had to breathe *Let go* and he would, so why was she sitting there, her eyes holding his, her lips parted in appeal as a male hand smoothed up her arm to touch the bare curve of her shoulder?

'Say no once more, that's all,' Baxter urged, giving her the script so they could stop this madness before it really began.

She tried, licking dry lips as she raised shaking hands to his chest. But speaking seemed pointless when her heart— or was it his?—was beating like thunder, above which no sound was likely to be heard. And how could she push him away when her hands were sliding over muscle and sinew, already damp with perspiration, and the warmth of him was seeping into her senses, making her weak?

He held her there with magnetic blue eyes, mirroring her awakened feelings. What was happening to them both?

He stroked her cheek with the palm of his hand, the gentlest of gestures, and she turned her head until her lips pressed on his skin. She didn't know what to do next, but he did.

He moved his hand and traced the outline of her soft mouth.

She parted her lips and swallowed hard as his fingers slipped slowly inside, then out. It left her mouth moist, like a kiss, only more intimate, more sensual. No one had ever done such a thing to her before.

Her breath caught, and she stared at him with a mixture of pleasure and shock.

Baxter was left wondering if she was as experienced as she'd implied. His conscience told him to back off now, but her mouth told him something else as it came up to meet his, opening like a flower needing sun.

Dee barely understood what was happening. She had kissed boys, and been kissed by a man she'd grown to hate. But it had never been like this—a sweet drug rushing straight to the senses. Pure desire. Waves of it. Rising higher and higher, then falling—falling with him onto the bed, being held, stroked, pleasured. Holding close, closer, hands smoothing over his bare back, hard with muscle, sleek with sweat.

Hands pushing up her shirt, smoothing over her belly where desire kicked, spreading upwards. Hands on her breast, stroking, knowing—fingers, then mouth, suddenly on flesh that had never been kissed, tongue making sweet circles till it swelled for him and her body arched.

Baxter told himself she knew what she was doing, that she wanted him the way he wanted her—badly. He slid his hand down to the damp triangle between her thighs, but when he touched her there she suddenly went rigid.

He tried to ignore it, covering her mouth with his once more. She kissed him back, still warm and willing, but now those doubts wouldn't go away. He took her hand and, testing her, guided her towards him.

Dee felt him through the cloth of his jeans, and was shocked by her own reaction. She'd read magazines and knew all the mechanics of sex, but the reality was turning out to be something else.

She realised he wanted her to touch him. Wasn't that what couples did? Pleasure each other? Part of her wanted to do it. Part just couldn't. She tried. She laid a nervous hand on his trousers and spread her fingers on his groin. It drew a strange, convulsive response from him, but not the desired one, and he suddenly stopped kissing her and, releasing her abruptly, sat up.

Dee lay where she was, coping with a confusion of emotions—longing, bewilderment, shame. What had she done wrong?

Baxter held her eyes for a brief moment, saw the truth in them and wondered at his own sanity. He reached down to pull the striped shirt past her hips, as if he could somehow undo the damage, but she rolled away, then edged to the far side of the bed.

Dee hoped he would just go.

Instead he appeared next to her, and laid a detaining hand on her arm when she would have run away again.

'You haven't done this before, have you?'

Dee's face burned. Was it so obvious?

'Who said I had?' she muttered back.

'I thought you and your stepfather...' He saw her stiffen, and didn't complete that particular sentence. 'Obviously I was mistaken. You should have told me. If I'd not realised and just carried on—'

'Well, you didn't!' Dee cut in, voice raw, her sense of rejection all too painfully transparent.

He understood only too well, replying softly, 'I had to stop. It wasn't personal to you...'

'Right!' A scathing glance from Dee told him she might be easy but she was nobody's fool.

'It wasn't,' he repeated. 'In fact, if you knew anything about men, you'd know how hard it was for me to stop when I did... It's just that deflowering virgins isn't something with which I'm particularly comfortable,' he admitted.

Dee felt herself blush to the roots of her hair. Did he have to be so blunt?

'You're a very bright, very pretty girl, and you deserve better than this,' he went on, softening the message slightly. 'Your first time should be special. With a boy of your own age, not a man a decade too old for you... You must see that?'

He was waiting for an answer so Dee nodded. She realised one thing at least. He wouldn't leave her until he was sure she was all right about what had happened between them.

She nodded, though she wasn't all right. She nodded so he would go before she broke down again.

But Baxter wasn't so easily convinced. 'You're shaking.'

'I'm cold.' She wrapped her arms about her. She was suddenly chilled to the bone.

He stood and pulled loose the heavily patterned weave that covered the bed, revealing clean white sheets and a single blanket. He helped her between the sheets.

Dee lay there with her teeth chattering. She wondered if she was sick. She felt sick. As if she had the flu and wanted to die.

'I'll get some more covers.' He fetched a quilt from the blanket box at the end of the bed and draped it over her, then he touched her forehead.

Dee revived sufficiently to mutter, 'Leave me alone.'

'You may have a temperature,' he observed.

'I don't care; just stop playing doctor.' She turned from him and drew the covers almost over her head.

Effectively excluded, Baxter knew there was little else he could do. In fact, hadn't he done enough already? He'd taken in this damaged girl and then proceeded to damage her further. Some doctor he was. Just as well he wasn't hers.

Dee shut her eyes tight, and longed for him to go. She heard him walk round the bed to switch off the lamp at her side. It plunged the room into darkness. He walked away, and she waited to hear the door click shut behind him. Instead she heard the creak of a chair.

She lay there, aware of him still in the room. She felt no fear, just frustration. She might have cried out her emotions, but she couldn't now. Not while he was watching over her.

For how could she cry at his rejection when he had never really accepted her? He had made that so clear. His sexuality was no longer in doubt. The real problem lay with her. She was a girl, and he had wanted a woman.

That was what had saved her. Nothing else. There had

been no protestations from her. No attempt to hold onto her innocence.

For Baxter Ross, she was a push-over. For Baxter Ross, she had no pride.

But why? He didn't say nice things. He didn't tell her she was beautiful as others had. He didn't make promises. He hardly spoke at all.

Yet she had lain in his bed and let him hold her and touch her with his cool hands and his warm mouth, and she had wanted it all.

She shut her eyes, but she could still feel the touch of him, the glide of sweat and skin, the heat of their tangled bodies.

Absurd.

CHAPTER EIGHT

MOTES of dust hung in the shaft of sunlight that slashed a diagonal from the high tower window to Dee's bed.

She blinked sleep out of her eyes, but it wasn't the light that had roused her.

'Sorry, did I wake you?' A woman stood at the far end of the bed.

Dee studied her briefly. 'You must be Baxter's sister.'

'Guilty as charged.' A smile broke across a face that was a female version of his. 'And you are?'

She waited expectantly, intrigued rather than critical.

'A friend,' Dee volunteered limply.

'Yes, I guessed that.' Amused eyes took in Dee's scattered clothing and the man's shirt she was using as nightwear. She added it to the fact that Dee was in her brother's bed and asked, 'Is he in the bathroom?'

Dee shook her head and glanced towards the chair by the wall. Of course he wasn't there now, but he had been last night. He'd fallen asleep in the chair and she'd climbed out of bed to drape a blanket over him.

The blanket was still on the chair, but he must have woken and left some time in the night.

'I think he's upstairs,' she informed his sister, 'in the spare room.'

'Oh, right.' His sister seemed to be mentally reassessing the situation. 'Sorry,' she smiled.

Sorry for her thoughts? Sorry for imagining Dee and Baxter were lovers?

'My name's Catriona—Cat for short,' she introduced herself.

'I'm Dee—short for Deborah,' Dee volunteered in reply.

'Nice to meet you. Is that your dog, by the way? The one in the kitchen?'

'Yes. Is he all right?'

'Seems it. He is okay with children, I assume? I left my daughter stroking him while my husband takes things in from the car.'

'Morag.' Dee recalled the name.

'Yes. Baxter's told you about us?'

'A little.'

'Well, I can't say he's returned the compliment.' Cat Macdonald pulled a slight face. 'He can be singularly uncommunicative, my brother.'

Tell me about it, Dee could have said, but confined herself to a brief, polite smile.

'Unless, of course…' His sister clapped a surprised hand over her mouth. 'Gracious, he hasn't done it, has he? I don't believe it!'

'Done what?' Dee was uncertain what she should admit to his sister.

Cat Macdonald became hesitant too, then switched to saying, 'Do you know about Joseph, the African boy Baxter's sponsoring?'

Dee answered with a nod, though she hadn't known Joseph was African.

'A bit.' she replied circumspectly.

'He's only eighteen.' Being in her late thirties, Cat obviously shared her brother's view on age. Eighteen was still a boy to her. 'How old are you?'

She studied Dee's face and began to frown. Fresh from sleep, Dee had lost the dark circles round her eyes and some of her pallor, and there wasn't a line on her face.

'Almost eighteen,' she replied defensively.

'Oh, Lord!' Cat Macdonald's eyes went heavenward while she shook her head. 'Well, I suppose you have to be young to be convincing, but I still think it's crazy, and I'm going to tell him so.'

'Him,' of course, was Baxter, but what was 'it'? Was Cat aware of his marriage plans?

'I think he's changed his mind,' Dee volunteered, although she wasn't altogether sure if they were talking about the same thing.

'Well, thank God for that!' his sister exclaimed with relief, which was short-lived as she questioned Dee's presence. 'But, if that's the case, why bring you up here?'

Good question. Dee didn't exactly have an answer.

'I've injured my leg.' It was the only reason Dee could come up with.

'Right,' Cat Macdonald said, but sounded equally unconvinced. 'I think I'd better go up and talk to him... I'm sorry to have disturbed you, by the way,' she added at the door. 'We saw the car and assumed Baxter would be up and around.'

'We arrived very late.' And got to sleep even later, Dee recalled with a blush. 'What time is it?'

'Nearly twelve,' his sister informed her as she left the room. 'But don't worry, I'll make lunch for us all.'

Dee forced a smile in return, then dropped back on the bed and emitted a groan. After last night, she could barely face Baxter Ross again, far less his whole tribe. Not that his sister seemed unlikeable. In fact, she seemed a considerably warmer human being than her brother. But Dee really had no place in this family reunion.

She saw that she had two options. Either she feigned illness and remained in bed, or she got up and went out.

Up and out struck her as safer, so Dee shuffled to the edge of the bed and carefully tested her weight on her bad knee. It was sore, but bearable.

Her few belongings were in Baxter's car, so she had no choice but to dress in yesterday's clothes. Unwilling to use dirty underwear, she took a pair of boxer shorts from his drawer. They were huge on her, and in danger of falling down, but she zipped her jeans over them, then drew her belt tight round her small waist. She'd still been wearing his leather jacket last night, and she put it on now over her thin T-shirt.

She descended to the kitchen to find Henry. He was stretched out beside an Aga cooker, which was the only period feature in a modernised room with fitted units of plain wood and a long breakfast bar. At it, perched on a stool, sat a bright-eyed girl of about five years old.

'Hi.' Dee greeted the child and her parents. There was no sign of Baxter.

'This is Dee.' Cat introduced her to the man chopping vegetables at the sink. 'Dee, this is Ewan, my husband.'

'And slave,' the man added wryly. 'Pleased to meet you, Dee.'

Dee exchanged smiles with Ewan, and hid her surprise at his age. He looked many years older than his wife.

'I'm Morag,' a voice piped up, and, before Dee had a chance to say anything, then asked, 'Why are you wearing Uncle Baxie's jacket?'

A brief, embarrassed silence followed before her mother scolded, 'Don't be silly, darling. It just looks like his jacket.'

'It *is* his jacket,' this precocious infant insisted. 'It's the one he wore at Christmas time... Don't you have one of your own?' she directed at Dee with innocent curiosity.

'Actually, no,' Dee responded. 'Mine was stolen. Your uncle's let me borrow his till I get a new one.'

'Like sharing,' the girl nodded solemnly. 'I don't like sharing, but Mum says if I don't learn to share I'll grow up into a horrible girl that no one will play with... Will you play with me?'

'I...um...have to walk the dog.' Dee made up the excuse quickly.

'Maybe later, darling.' Her mother made an apologetic face at Dee.

'But Uncle Baxie'll be awake later, and I'll be playing with him,' the little girl reasoned, before her father offered a distraction by picking her up and tickling her.

'Spoilt, that's the trouble,' Cat Macdonald confided to Dee. 'Her father's doing, of course.'

'I can see that.' Dee watched Ewan Macdonald swing his daughter into his arms, and she had a sudden, sharp recollection of another little girl being indulged by a loving older father.

She didn't realise her sadness showed till Cat Macdonald asked, 'Are you all right?'

'Yes, fine.' She just needed to get away from this happy family scene. 'Come on, Henry.'

She patted her leg and the dog reluctantly came to heel. She took hold of his collar and murmured a quick farewell.

Cat Macdonald followed her onto the landing, observing her limp. 'Are you sure you're fit enough?'

'I'm fine. The knee's just a little stiff.' Dee minimised the injury.

The other woman still looked unsure. 'How long will you be? Baxter may be concerned when he wakens.'

'He won't worry,' Dee stated confidently. 'He knows I can take care of myself.'

Cat Macdonald was left wondering what exactly that meant, but gave up arguing. 'Yes, well, don't go too far. There's a path leading up the hill. You can let him run there.'

'Thanks.' Dee didn't point out that Henry's running days were over, but exchanged smiles with the other woman before continuing downstairs.

She took her time, both for her own sake and the old dog's, whose joints were stiff. Of course, Baxter Ross couldn't be like any normal person and live in a normal house—preferably a bungalow.

Still, when she eventually got outside and stood back from his tower, she could almost see its attraction. Banked by moorland on one side, with grass fields and a river on the other, it was the ideal place for someone who liked privacy.

There was no other habitation in sight. If Dee wanted to reach civilisation, she would have to walk to it. With only a half-formed plan in mind, she went to the hired car first. Behind it stood a Volvo and behind that an Audi, presumably belonging to his sister and brother-in-law.

Baxter had left the hire-car open, and she took it as a good sign. She rifled through the case on the back seat and shoved some bare essentials into her rucksack. She kept on his jacket, knowing she might need it at night, and, retrieving Henry's lead from the boot, set off.

The track was made of earth and loose stone, and maintained to a minimum standard only. She walked a good fifteen minutes before she reached a road. It was a very minor road, with no signposts and no real promise of a bustling metropolis at the end, but Dee reasoned it must lead somewhere.

She crossed to the far verge to face oncoming traffic, and walked down rather than up. It was hard going and quite dangerous with so many bends in the road, and Scotland in July was almost as warm as London had been. After half an hour's walking, she was sweating, Henry was panting, her knee was throbbing and she had arrived nowhere of significance.

She crossed back to the other side, sat on a grassy knoll off the road, and tried hitching. Unfortunately there were no dog or people lovers in the rare cars that appeared. She could have cried. She did cry. With pure frustration. In her desperation to get away from Baxter Ross and his family, she had stranded herself and Henry in the middle of nowhere.

Worse, with nothing to do but sit at the roadside, she had given herself too much opportunity to relive last night over and over, like a blue movie in her head.

She wanted to tell herself that was why she was running—in disgust. The problem was her one great virtue: she was almost *always* honest with herself. She could rerun the movie a dozen times, but she couldn't freeze-frame it at any point where she'd said no. She had been willing, and he had stopped. Virgins weren't his thing.

She should have been grateful. She *was* grateful. She had fought Edward to keep her virginity, and lost her home over it. She didn't want to squander it on a man to whom she meant little. So why had she let her guard down at all?

Baxter Ross didn't mean that much to her, did he? She barely knew him, and she didn't believe one could love a virtual stranger. No, love didn't come into it.

Dee shook her head. She couldn't figure it out. Much wiser to run, then analyse at a distance—only a mile down the road was hardly that much of a distance.

Hope revived briefly as a car came round the corner and pulled up on the verge beside her. It died as the driver got out.

'Dee?' Cat's expression was all concern. 'We were worried when you were gone so long. Is it your leg?'

'Yes,' Dee lied.

'Baxter said you couldn't go far,' Cat ran on. 'He's gone out looking for you on foot.'

She helped Dee up and into the passenger seat of the Volvo, before stowing Henry in the boot.

Dee wasn't given much chance to object but, when Cat climbed in herself, she asked, 'Could you take me to the nearest town?'

'Linlithgow?'

'Wherever.'

Scottish geography wasn't Dee's strong point, but it sounded like somewhere she should have heard of. 'I need a few things,' she added rather lamely.

Cat looked at her closely, before murmuring, 'I think we should go home first, don't you?'

She didn't wait for a response but, reversing into a field, returned the way they'd come.

Dee realised how pathetic her escape attempt had been. A couple of minutes' drive and she was back where she'd started.

Ewan Macdonald was waiting at the door of the tower, and, after a quick word with Cat, left in his Audi.

Dee felt guilty as she learned her disappearance had delayed his departure for a meeting. From their brief exchange, Dee gathered Ewan Macdonald was a businessman of some kind.

She was made to feel guiltier as Cat went ahead of her, saying, 'I'll just go check on Morag, then try to reach Baxter on his mobile to tell him I've found you.'

Dee was meant to follow, but she remained by the door, reluctant to go inside.

A minute or two later the older woman returned.

'I spoke to Baxter,' she relayed to Dee. 'He was very relieved to hear you were all right. He's walked up to the crag, so it'll be a while before he's back… I'm to keep you from running away again,' she added with a small laugh.

Dee didn't laugh back. In fact, her expression must have been all too readable.

'You really were running away,' Cat concluded for herself.

'Sort of,' Dee admitted.

'From Baxter or the situation?'

Baxter, Dee could have said, but she didn't want to give the wrong impression. 'He hasn't harmed me. I just don't think I should stick around.'

'You could be right,' Cat actually conceded. 'I admire my brother both as a man and a doctor, but this latest scheme of his is just too risky. The whole idea of an arranged marriage...' She shook her head at it. 'I know Baxter feels he has an obligation to fulfil, but there must be some other way of doing it... And you've obviously had second thoughts.'

'Yes,' Dee agreed, confused by the rest.

What obligation? And to whom? The aunt who'd left him something in her will, she supposed.

'Well, don't worry, I won't let him force you into anything,' Cat assured her. 'For now, why don't you have lunch? Everyone else has eaten, but we left some for you.'

'Thanks.' A resigned Dee followed the other woman up the spiral staircase.

Cat served her a pasta dish with chicken and courgettes. After a diet of fry-ups, it was haute cuisine.

The other woman busied herself in the kitchen while Dee ate, but Morag insisted on staring at her from the far end of the table.

This, it seemed, was the prelude to being interviewed.

'What's your dog called?'

'Henry.'

A pert nose was wrinkled. 'That's not what I'd call one. If I had a dog, I'd call it Belle.'

'That's nice, too,' Dee smiled back.

'I wanted a dog,' she then confided to Dee. 'But Mummy's having a baby instead.'

'Really?' Dee said, feeling awkward.

But Morag's mother was seemingly used to the child's forthrightness, and smiled as she patted her slight bulge. 'Yes, and not before time, too.' She shook her head at her precocious first-born, and said, 'Only children can be a handful in their own way.'

'Yes,' Dee agreed politely.

'Have you a sister?' Morag asked of Dee.

'No. No brothers either,' she admitted. 'And your mum's right—I think it's much better to have some. I wish I had.'

'Oh.' Morag thought about this for a moment. 'Never mind. You and Uncle Baxie can have lots of babies.'

It came from nowhere, and left Dee almost choking on a piece of chicken.

This time Cat Macdonald turned completely from the sink, an appalled look on her face. 'Morag! Whatever makes you say such a thing?'

Morag was unfazed. 'I heard you tell Daddy earlier that Dee wasn't too young to get married if that's what she wanted.'

'Honestly, darling, you must stop listening in to adults' conversations.' Cat sighed heavily. 'That's why you get so mixed up. Dee may get married, yes, but it won't be to Uncle Baxie… Heavens, no!' She dismissed the very idea with a laugh.

'Then who?' the child asked.

Good question. Dee waited, jaw dropped, for the answer.

It came slowly, reluctantly. 'Well, it's just a possibility that Dee'll marry Joseph.'

'Joseph?' the child echoed in surprise.

Joseph? Dee just mouthed the word, but her reaction was nearer shock. Baxter wanted her to marry Joseph? Not him? Of course. It had never been him!

'But it may not happen,' mother stressed to daughter, catching Dee's deepening frown.

'Why not?' Morag enquired. 'I like Joseph. He makes me laugh. What colour will their babies be?'

'Morag!' Her mother shot her a silencing look so fierce it actually worked, and added sternly, 'Why don't you go to the toilet?'

'I don't need it.'

'Go anyway.'

Morag was helped up from her chair and firmly shooed out of the door.

Only then did Cat continue. 'I really am sorry about this. She's obsessed with babies at the moment, and I can't really explain to her about you and Joseph. I mean, the less people who know about it and all that, you understand?'

No, but Dee was beginning to. What possible reason could Baxter Ross have for paying her to marry a complete stranger? One who came from Africa. She could think of only one.

'When does Joseph's visa expire?' She tried out her theory.

And Cat Macdonald proved it, responding, 'I'm not sure. Baxter brought him over on a temporary visa last Christmas, and he's tried to gain him student status ever since. But that route's hit complications... I really thought he was joking when he suggested getting a British bride for him, but evidently not.' Her eyes rested on Dee, leaving her in no doubt who that bride was to be.

'Why does he want to help Joseph so much?' she asked.

'He promised Joseph's parents he'd take care of him,' Cat Macdonald explained. 'They both died while working in a hospital Baxter was overseeing. Some kind of fever. Baxter was seriously ill, too... But that's had its compensations.'

'Compensations?' Dee frowned.

'The fever's left him prone to infection,' Cat explained, 'which is why he's finally given up field work.'

'How does he feel about that?' Dee enquired.

Cat shrugged. 'I haven't had the chance to ask him. I'm just glad he's out of it before he gets his head blown off... Maybe now he can settle down and concentrate on living a halfway normal life,' she reflected in dry tones.

Dee wondered what his sister had in mind for him, but didn't ask. It wasn't her business. None of it was.

When Morag reappeared, Dee took the chance to say, 'If you don't mind, I'd like to go for a lie down.'

'Yes, of course,' Catriona replied, but she was hesitant.

Dee, who wasn't up to any more dashes for freedom, added, 'I'll leave Henry down here, if that's okay.'

'Yes, fine.' The older woman was reassured by the sight of the old dog stretched out by the Aga.

Dee departed, leaving Morag asking her mother what was wrong with her leg.

She mounted the stairs slowly, her knee aching with each

step. Her 'walk' hadn't improved her condition. In fact, she
suspected the knee was swollen with fluid once more.

Although the tower was cool, she felt hot and sticky. She
emptied her rucksack on the bed and sorted through underwear and T-shirts, finding something suitable to wear. She
washed in the washbasin rather than shower, because she
didn't want the bandage to need changing again. She
emerged, scrubbed and shiny, and fortunately fully clothed,
to find Baxter Ross prowling the bedroom.

She hadn't expected it so she wasn't ready for him. That
was what she reasoned later. At the time she just stood
there, breath catching, heart stopping at the very sight of
him.

In fantasy he would have held out his arms and she
would have run to him, laughing. In reality he strode up to
her, giving her no chance to run, laugh or even draw breath.

'Where the hell were you going?' he demanded without
preamble.

'I...a walk... I—I went for a walk,' she stammered,
shocked by his anger.

'With a rucksack full of clothes?' he threw back. 'Don't
take me for a fool. Where were you heading?'

'I've no idea!' She mustered up her own temper. 'Anywhere but here would have done!'

'Because of last night?' he countered.

She felt her face flame.

'I told you—it won't happen again,' he ground out. 'God
knows why it happened at all!'

His eyes flicked over her—face scrubbed, skin rosy,
looking more twelve than seventeen.

'I'm so repulsive, am I?' Dee concluded from his manner. 'Well, thanks, that just makes me feel *so* much better.'

'I didn't mean it that way,' he replied heavily. 'You must
know you can turn a few heads, even with the haircut and
ear armour...' Baxter paused for a moment, realising finally
what had been different about her last night. The earrings
had gone, leaving only the puncture marks where they'd
been.

'Anyway—' he refocused his thoughts '—how attractive
you are isn't the issue. The point is,' he laboured on, 'I am

not your stepfather. I don't chase after girls young enough to be my daughter.'

Well, it was honest. Too honest. Dee felt rejected rather than reassured.

'You weren't so scrupulous last night,' she said, out of hurt and an odd sense of despair.

'No, I wasn't,' he agreed heavily. 'I was tired after a long journey and a rough week. I'm barely getting my head round being back in so-called civilisation. Add that to a year's abstinence, and it seems I can behave as badly as the next man. I'm not asking you to forgive, just under-stand—'

Oh, she did. Only too well!

'You wanted sex to wind down from a stressful week, and were randy enough not to care about the date on my birth certificate,' Dee cut in, out-franking his frankness. 'But you got cold feet when I turned out not to be quite the easy lay you thought I was... Have I missed out any-thing?'

Nothing. She had summed up last night from a viewpoint so cynical it was hard to believe she *was* still fundamentally innocent.

It saddened rather than angered Baxter as he recalled the girl in the photograph he'd seen yesterday. A beautiful girl, she'd smiled out at the world with a clear gaze and a face full of expectation. What had happened to her?

'It really wasn't like that,' he finally replied. 'My actions were certainly inexcusable, but they were also unplanned. And I have absolutely never thought of you in such terms.'

He spoke with a quiet sincerity that undermined Dee's own anger, and made her wish that things could be right between them once more.

'Honestly?' she murmured back.

'Honestly,' Baxter echoed, then mused aloud, 'In fact, far from being experienced, I wonder if you even know when you're being provocative.'

'Provocative?' She looked genuinely surprised at the word.

Which proved his point, somewhat. 'It's obviously not intentional,' he was quick to add. 'You're just...well...a shade outspoken. I'll probably get used to it, but I wouldn't recommend your being quite so—let's say—upfront with other men. They might get the wrong idea.'

Dee could have chosen to flare up again. She could have told him he was the only man to whom she'd reacted in this way. But she took his advice instead and kept quiet, and gave a vague nod, acknowledging the fact that right or wrong it was well-meant.

He nodded, too, as if they'd reached an agreement, and their gazes held a moment or two longer before both looked away to break eye contact.

'Right.' His tone became more businesslike. 'Now we've got that out of the way, do you feel you could stay?'

They were to return to an impersonal relationship. That was the agenda. Only Dee wasn't sure if she could.

'On what basis?' she asked at length.

Baxter's mouth thinned. She wasn't going to make this easy. Perhaps he should just let her go.

'You are currently homeless, you have an injured knee and you have no source of income,' he spelled out. 'Three good reasons to stay, I'd have said.'

Dee could think of some equally good reasons to go. It had taken months to toughen up to life on the streets. How was she going to feel after a few weeks in his ivory tower? Too scared to leave?

'That depends on the pay-back,' she countered.

'I've already told you, last night was—' he began heavily.

'Not that,' she cut across him. 'The reason you got me up here in the first place.'

He frowned convincingly.

She hummed the 'Wedding March' in flat, ironic tones. 'Or were you going to wait a week or two to spring it on me?'

He shook his head. 'Rest assured, there's no question of an arranged marriage between us.'

'Oh, I know that,' Dee seethed as he continued to play her for a fool. 'I meant between me and your native friend from Kirundi.'

If she'd intended to annoy him, she succeeded, as he

clipped back, 'Don't be so English and ignorant. My *native* friend is a highly intelligent young man descended from African princes. Normally *he* wouldn't look twice at *you.*'

And that's me told, Dee thought, with no ready answer back. She hadn't intended to sound prejudiced. Her objections had really been to Baxter Ross's duplicity.

'And, as I've already told you,' he grated on, 'I have shelved any plans for an arranged marriage between *you* and anyone.'

Because she couldn't be relied on, Dee assumed. Or trusted not to talk. For surely it was illegal to broker a marriage for someone to gain British citizenship?

'I wouldn't tell anyone,' she found herself saying.

'It's not that simple,' he went on. 'Marry a temporary resident like Joseph and the Home Office would descend on you. It wouldn't be a matter of not telling. You'd have to convince them that your relationship is real, that you're deeply in love with a man you've barely met, and that you really intend spending the rest of your life with him.'

'I could do that,' Dee claimed. 'Well…if I wanted to.'

It elicited a sceptical sound from Baxter Ross. 'Yes, I can just imagine you playing the doting wife. The Home Office would have to be wearing rose-coloured spectacles if they were to detect any air of romance about you.'

'Oh, and you're a judge of that, are you?' Dee was stung into retorting. 'The last of the great romantics? Scotland's answer to Don Juan. An expert on affairs of the heart as well as its internal workings—'

'All right, all right.' He raised a hand, accepting her point. 'I wasn't setting myself up as an authority. I wasn't even criticising. I was just stating a fact—you're not the type to be swept off her feet so you're hardly likely to know how to act like that…

And besides, you'd have to learn every detail of Joseph's life—you'd have to spend long periods of time in his company and be seen to do so, you'd have to face any racial prejudice coming your way because he's black—'

'I don't get you.' She interrupted this list of negatives. 'Why are you trying to put me off, when not three days ago you were willing to pay me megabucks for doing it?'

'*You* changed your mind, remember?' he threw back at her.

'Actually, I didn't,' Dee finally admitted. 'The truth is I slept in. By the time I got to the Continental, you'd left.'

He looked unconvinced. 'You didn't tell me that when I saw you later.'

'No, well, I was too busy nursing an injury,' she reminded him in turn. 'Having been rugby tackled.'

He pulled a face. 'How is it, by the way, your knee?'

'Fine!'

'I doubt it, after your escapade earlier,' he said in disapproving tones.

He was right, of course. Her knee was throbbing. But she wasn't about to strip off to play doctors with him.

She got in first, 'I don't want you looking at it.'

'I wasn't going to,' he stated, 'but you'll need to see someone tomorrow. I'll arrange for Cat to take you into Linlithgow, then you can catch a train to Edinburgh and beyond if you choose.'

'Is that what you want?' She challenged this sudden offer of helpful information.

He shook his head. 'You're not fit for travelling or sleeping rough, and I have enough people on my conscience already.'

Dee wondered what he meant, and dared to ask, 'Is this Joseph one of them?'

He hesitated, before replying, 'His parents are. I owe them, so I owe Joseph.'

'Cat said they died.'

'Yes.'

'Of some kind of fever?'

He nodded, then explained briefly, 'I oversaw a hospital they ran. The water became contaminated with a new strain of virus.'

'That doesn't sound like your fault,' she commented. 'Especially if you got ill, too.'

'My fault? Maybe not,' he conceded. 'But I was still responsible... Looking after Joseph is the least I can do.'

'Why didn't you tell me the truth instead of letting me

think you were after some legacy?' To Dee's mind the truth showed him in a much better light.

He shrugged. 'You seemed to like the legacy version—and it *was* actually your invention.'

Was it? Dee supposed it might have been. But he'd been quite happy leaving her with the wrong conclusion. It was almost as if he liked people thinking the worst of him.

She watched as he walked towards the dresser and began to open and shut drawers, moving the contents either onto the bed or into a drawer below the wardrobe.

'You can use this dresser,' he instructed when he'd finished. 'And the tallboy, of course.'

'You shouldn't have bothered.' She hadn't realised he was clearing space for her. 'I don't have much.'

'Your mother may send on the rest of your things,' he relayed to her. 'She asked for my address and I gave it.'

'Oh,' Dee murmured, but was still puzzled about something. 'Yesterday, I thought you were taking me back to London.'

'I was,' he confirmed. 'I changed my mind.'

Dee's frown deepened. When he didn't volunteer more, she prompted, 'Why?'

He thought for a moment, then dryly admitted, 'I have absolutely no idea.'

Dee stared at him in surprise. He hadn't struck her as the impulsive type—more cool and calculating.

'Anyway, whether she sends them or not,' he continued, 'you'll need more clothes if you intend staying for a while.'

How can I stay after last night? she might have asked. But it seemed last night was no big deal to him.

'I'll make do,' she shrugged.

'If money's the problem, I can let you have some.' His attitude was casual, but Dee was still left feeling like a charity case.

'I won't take money from you.' The stubborn note in her voice told him she was serious.

'Okay, when your knee's mended you can earn it,' he countered.

'How?'

'I don't know... Can you cook?'

The suggestion didn't offend Dee, but she felt she should be honest. 'Well, I could give it a stab.'

'Ah, right…not such a clever idea,' he concluded from her answer.

'I could clean,' she offered.

He looked surprised. 'You'd do that?'

'Well, it's hardly my life's ambition,' she remarked dryly. 'But neither's begging in tube stations.'

'Busking,' Baxter corrected for once, and drew a fleeting smile to her face, before asking, 'So what is?'

'What is what?'

'Your life's ambition?'

Dee considered her reply. 'I don't think I had one. I just assumed it would be A levels, then university.'

'That still must be possible,' he commented. 'Your mother said you were a high achiever at school.'

Dee shrugged. It wasn't exactly modesty. School just seemed a long time distant.

'When I get settled.' It was what she told herself.

Maybe he saw it as an excuse, because he said, 'Joseph commutes to college in Edinburgh on a daily basis.'

'Yes, well, I'm not going to be around long enough, am I?' she pointed out, resenting the comparison with his protégé.

'No, probably not,' he conceded, then seemed to grow tired of the conversation. He added, 'I'm driving into the city now to return the hire-car. Is there anything I can get you? Soap? Toothbrush? Women's things?'

'A single to London?' Dee added flippantly.

He didn't laugh. 'Yes, if that's what you want,' he replied coldly. 'You're not a prisoner here.'

He was making it easy for her. No need for any more abortive attempts to limp and hitch to the nearest town. He would drive her. He would buy her a ticket.

So why did she say, 'I'll hang around for a day or two, if it's all the same to you.'

'It is.' He was indifferent, able to walk away—as he did now, without a backward glance.

He left the door ajar and she heard his footsteps ringing

on the stone, the shutting and opening of doors and voices from the floor below.

She went out to the keep window on her own landing, and looked below. She saw him emerge from the tower with his niece Morag hanging onto his arm, dancing to keep up with him and chattering nineteen to the dozen.

Dee wondered if the adoration was one-sided, until she saw him bend to pick her up and swirl her around. Cries of 'Again, again,' followed each time he put her down, and the serious child of earlier was transformed into a giggler.

The child climbed into his car with him as her mother fetched a booster seat from the back of her car. Then Cat got behind the driving wheel of her Volvo and followed Baxter down the drive. Presumably he was going to get a lift back from his sister after he'd disposed of the hire-vehicle.

Alone now, Dee lay down on the bed, tired once more, but sleep wouldn't come. Instead she watched the pattern of light and shadow from the two great windows set high in the wall, and tried not to think of anything.

It didn't work. It was like a seed that had taken root and was now growing like a creeper. Every branch, every thought led back to him.

He had done her no favours. Through him she had damaged her knee, lost her squat and almost given away what little she had left of her self-respect. In return he had offered her the chance of earning some dodgy money, doing something that was undoubtedly illegal and quite possibly carried with it a jail sentence.

As Sir Galahads went, he was more a knight in tarnished armour.

So why was she lying here, after barely three days' acquaintance—much of it spent arguing and fighting—with an absolute conviction that she had met the man she wanted to be with for the rest of her life?

It was crazy. She was mad. And he didn't give a damn. Just perfect!

CHAPTER NINE

DEE drifted off to sleep and was woken early evening by Cat Macdonald. Dinner was being served in the great hall. Dee might have declined if she hadn't been so hungry. Cat left her to dress.

She washed first, then put back on her jeans and T-shirt. Her leg was better for being rested, but she still had to limp her way down the spiral staircase.

The great hall, she remembered, was on the landing opposite the kitchen. It lived up to its name—an immense room with a huge fireplace at one end flanked by dark blue armchairs and a long tartan sofa. At the other end the Macdonald family and Baxter were already seated on studded leather seats at an antique oak table.

She slipped into a vacant chair at the opposite end to Baxter. She felt a stranger in the midst of this family gathering, but the Macdonalds seemed perfectly at ease with her presence. Perhaps she was the latest in a long line of females to grace this table.

Perhaps that was Baxter's usual pattern—to come back home with some female in tow, enjoy a brief affair, no strings attached, then return abroad.

Dee told herself it was none of her business, but spent much of the meal contemplating what kind of woman would be his normal companion. Mature? Sophisticated? Experienced? Probably all three, and beautiful and bright for good measure. What chance did she stand?

None.

He barely looked at her during the meal, and she trained herself not to look at him. She kept silent rather than draw attention to herself—which was easy enough, because Cat and Morag were great talkers, and even Ewan was too, when he got into his stride.

Dinner was over and Morag asleep on a couch by the

fire when Cat Macdonald finally observed, 'You're very quiet, Dee. Is your knee hurting?'

'No, it's fine…thank you,' she responded politely.

'Possibly she finds us all a bit overpowering,' Ewan suggested.

'A little, yes,' Dee admitted.

'What's your own family like?' asked Cat.

Dee pulled a face. How did she describe her family? Non-existent?

Baxter did it for her, saying, 'Dysfunctional.'

'Oh,' Cat murmured sympathetically, then tried hard not to look curious, but didn't quite manage it. 'And have you been away from home long?'

'A while.' Dee really was reluctant to talk about this.

Baxter didn't share her reservations. 'Dee ran away to London at Easter and has been more or less homeless since.'

'Oh, dear.'

'She's been sleeping in doorways and squats.'

'How dreadful!'

Both Cat Macdonald and her husband turned pitying eyes on her.

Resenting it, Dee scowled at Baxter. 'Why don't you tell them about the begging and the stealing, too? Not to mention my life of prostitution!'

Two jaws dropped open while a third went rigid at her dramatics.

Baxter prompted her with a hard look, but she ignored it.

'Tell them the truth,' he ordered tersely.

'You're the one with verbal diarrhoea—you tell them,' she responded defiantly, unintimidated by his glower. 'And while you're at it why don't you get out your violin as well?'

Then she pushed herself away from the table and, in the deafening silence that followed, limped with as much dignity as she could muster to the door.

'Where are you going?' Baxter demanded, on his feet and oblivious to the shocked looks from his family. 'If you think I'm going to run after you another time—'

'I'm going to wash the dishes,' she snapped back. 'That's what we said. Cleaning in return for my keep.'

She didn't wait for a reply, but limped towards the kitchen, intending to do just what she said.

Buoyed up by temper and indignation, she was throwing plates and cutlery and glasses all in the same bowl when Cat Macdonald appeared.

Dee had half expected her brother, and her look was unintentionally fierce. Cat raised her hands in mock defence.

'Don't shoot, I'm only the messenger. My brother says you can't do the dishes, not with your bad knee.'

'He can tell me himself, if that's what he wants!'

'I think he's still counting to ten,' confided Cat, picking up a cloth to dry the dishes Dee was stacking. 'In fact, I haven't seen my brother this mad in a long time.'

'Good!' Dee said, but losing some of her righteous fury at Cat's amused manner. 'I suppose you think I'm behaving badly.'

'Well, if you are—' Cat smiled back '—I imagine you have your reasons.'

'It's just that I don't like him talking about me as if I'm some stray he's picked up.' Dee explained her indignation. 'I didn't ask for his help. I was doing perfectly all right. He practically kidnapped me.'

This rather extravagant claim drew a frown from Cat's face. 'You didn't agree to marry Joseph, then?'

'No. Yes. Sort of…' she answered in quick succession. 'He never told me about Joseph. I thought it was him I was meant to be marrying.'

'*Him?*' Cat repeated. 'Baxter, you mean?'

'Yes.'

'And you didn't mind that?'

'No,' Dee replied.

'Ri-ight.' Catriona Macdonald nodded in a knowing manner.

It took Dee a moment to realise what impression she'd given. 'Not because I fancied him or anything,' she denied quickly.

The other woman looked unconvinced, and Dee decided

it was time to tell the truth. So, out it came, the whole story, up to the point when they'd arrived at the tower in the early hours of that morning. Was it really less than a day?

When Dee had finished, Cat stood, shaking her head in disbelief. 'I can't decide who's crazier—you or my brother. Weren't you worried, going off like that with a virtual stranger? I mean, *I* know Baxter would never take advantage, but you weren't to know that.'

Dee supposed it had been extremely foolish, but at no time had she really worried that she would come to physical harm with Baxter Ross. Even last night, when things had threatened to get out of hand, he had behaved honourably.

'Right at the beginning, when we first met, I thought he was gay,' she explained.

This drew laughter. 'Baxter? Gay? Well, as his sister, I'm not privy to the intimacies of his relationships, but there's certainly been more than one woman sharing that four poster of his over the years.'

'Okay, it seems silly now,' Dee agreed. 'But he made this big thing about not being interested in young girls, and I misunderstood.'

'I imagine he was trying to reassure you,' Cat Macdonald concluded.

'Well, he could have been plainer,' Dee insisted, 'instead of letting me think what I liked.'

'Oh, that's just Baxter. He never discusses his private life.'

'Just other people's.'

Dee was still smarting from the way he'd talked of her. As though she was a charity case, some homeless kid he'd picked off the streets.

'He meant no offence, I'm sure, in giving us your background,' his sister assuaged.

'So you'd know who I was,' Dee went on. 'His good deed for the day!'

She spoke in a hard, hurt voice that must have betrayed more than she'd intended, because Catriona Macdonald's expression became contemplative rather than condemning.

'Dee...you haven't...well, fallen for my brother, have you?' she asked in worried tones.

Her kind eyes said more. They told Dee that such a falling promised only pain.

'No, of course not,' Dee denied, face hot. 'Don't be silly. It's ridiculous. I mean... *God, he's ancient!*' she added with feeling, desperate to throw Cat Macdonald off the track.

She obviously succeeded, as Cat smiled in relief and kept smiling, even when a throat was cleared in the background.

'Baxter.' His sister turned from the sink and acknowledged his presence in the open doorway. 'We were just talking about you.'

'So I heard.' His eyes travelled from her to Dee and stayed there.

'Cheer up, little brother.' Cat Macdonald tried to make light of the situation. 'Imagine how I feel. If you're ancient, I must be positively antediluvian,' she ran on, refusing to take insult. 'Anyway, she simply means you're too old for her, that's all.'

She laughed, expecting one or both to laugh with her, but they traded stares instead.

'It's what you said,' Dee finally remarked, on the defensive.

'Since when have you taken to listening to what I say?' he countered, unsmiling. 'She shouldn't be on that leg,' he directed at his sister. 'Did you tell her?'

'Come on, Baxter, lighten up—' Cat cajoled in return.

'Did you?' he repeated in hard tones.

'Yes, she did,' Dee interceded. 'So stop picking on her. Pick on me if you want to yell at someone.'

'All right, I will,' he responded, a nerve jumping at his temple. 'If you insist on being wilful, careless and downright stupid,' he threw at her, 'then don't blame me if your bloody leg swells up and drops off.'

'*Drops off?*' Dee echoed in scathing tones. 'Tell me, Doctor, is that some new medical term? Sounds very technical.'

'You want an exact prognosis?' he bit back.

'No,' she snapped in reply, 'because I wouldn't believe that either.'

They both forgot they had an audience until Cat Macdonald intoned, 'Seconds out. Round over. Back to your corners, please… And let's decide this by more rational means, perhaps?' she appealed, glancing from one angry face to another.

Her brother gave her a dark look for interfering, but said, 'You tell her, then. She's too pig-headed to listen to me. She has to give the knee a chance to heal unless she wants to end up with a permanent limp.'

'Did you catch that?' Cat directed at Dee.

'Yes,' Dee snapped. 'And could you please tell your brother that it's none of his business? He isn't my doctor and I don't want his phoney concern.'

'Okay,' Cat nodded. 'She says—'

'I heard!' Baxter cut across her. 'And it's just as well I'm not her doctor, because I know no cure for terminal stupidity!'

It was his parting shot as he turned on his heel and went through the door, slamming it behind him. The two women were left to stare in his wake.

Cat was more intrigued than disturbed. 'You certainly know how to make my brother lose his cool.'

'I suppose you're on his side,' Dee said, feeling sorry for herself.

'Normally,' Cat agreed. 'But on this one I think I'll stay on neutral ground… That said, maybe you should rest that leg. I can finish the dishes before I go.'

'Yes, all right.' Dee didn't want to argue with the other woman. 'Perhaps I'll have an early night.'

'Good idea,' Cat smiled. 'Things will seem clearer in the morning, but if you need someone to talk to give me a call and I'll come over.'

'Thanks, but I'll be fine,' she declared, to herself as much as Cat Macdonald. 'I'll just ignore him.'

'You do that,' Cat echoed as Dee limped out of the door.

Ignore him. It sounded impossible, but it turned out to be relatively simple. She went up to bed, tossed and turned for a few hours, then slept like the dead. By the time she woke, Baxter was gone.

She knew she was alone in the tower even before she found his note in the kitchen. No 'Dear Dee'. No 'Dear anything'. Just short and to the point: *Gone to the university. Back in the evening. Help yourself. B.*

Help herself to what? Dee wondered. The key on the table? The food in the fridge? The money laid out in full view on a work-surface? What?

She fingered the five twenty-pound notes. Enough for some new clothes. But also enough for a rail ticket. The choice was hers.

So she chose to leave the money where it was, and instead gave herself the grand tour of her new 'squat', first letting Henry out for a mooch around.

There wasn't much in the way of a garden, just rough grass that someone had cut, but it would have needed more attention to look healthy. A path at the back led to outbuildings. The first was a garage, now empty but presumably where he kept his car. The next was locked. She peered in through the window and saw what had to be a small sailing boat covered by a green tarpaulin. The final building was a store for garden tools, mower and work bench.

She returned to the house and decided to explore the ground floor. She pushed open a door that was obviously little used, because it creaked as it gave, and found herself standing in a large, resounding stone hall that had probably never been living quarters but rather a place for the storage of weapons or animals in more feudal days.

It had yet to be restored, and in places the inner walls had crumbled. She walked to the far end and discovered a chamber leading off. In the centre was a square man-sized hole with steps leading downwards. Dee craned her neck inside and saw the steps disappear into a room almost too low to stand in. She realised this must be the tower's dungeon, a black hole cut into the earth, with no ventilation to relieve the inevitable claustrophobia. The cruelty of past ages made her shiver, and she didn't dwell long in the room.

She knew both rooms on the next floor—the surprisingly

modern kitchen and the great hall which he used as dining
and living room. She looked round the latter again, ap-
praising his choice of furniture—heavy oak pieces to suit
its austere stone walls, dark rich velvet furnishings to offer
some comfort. It was a very masculine room, no woman's
touch anywhere.

She continued upstairs, by-passing Joseph's still unoc-
cupied room and her own, climbing the flight to the top
floor. It had only been partially renovated. She opened a
door into a bedroom with plastered walls, stained where
water had once penetrated from the roof above. It was furnished with odds and ends, including a single bed that
someone had roughly made.

She sat down on it to find the bed dipped in the middle.
She stretched out and found it short by a few inches. She
was tall but Baxter was taller, so it must be even shorter
for him. She told herself that no one had asked him to give
up his room, but felt guilty all the same.

She made up his bed properly—a skill she'd learned at
boarding school—and tidied up the clothes he'd left scattered round the room, before considering how wise that
was. She'd offered to clean for him, but maybe he would
wonder if she'd been prying.

On the same floor she found another attic bedroom, and
a study housing a desk that could barely be seen for the
papers scattered on top. She went no further than the door
of the study as that really would have been invading his
privacy.

Out on the landing again, she climbed a final set of steps,
narrow and airless and dark, ending at an overhead hatch.
She slid back a heavy bolt, pushed open the hatch and
scrambled out onto the flat roof and top ramparts of the
tower. With a good head for heights, she stayed up there
for a while, enjoying the sun on her face and the quite
breath-catching view.

She wondered if he had bought or inherited the tower. It
certainly fell into the category of unusual places to live.
But then there wasn't anything particularly usual about
Baxter Ross. She supposed its isolation suited him, al-

though, from what his sister had said, he didn't shun society altogether.

Dee again considered the kind of women he might like. Fellow world-savers? Career women? Intellectuals? Or was the primary qualification that they'd been alive for the first moon walk?

She had no feelings for these faceless women. She couldn't imagine he'd loved any, or they would be still here. She couldn't imagine him loving full stop. He was too contained, too remote, needing no one to survive.

He didn't expect love, didn't want it. And even if he had Dee was probably as far from his choice as any woman could be.

Dee told herself all this, but it made no difference.

When she heard a step on the stair late that afternoon, her heart was already in her mouth just waiting for the sight of him. When the kitchen door opened, her face fell.

'Do not be afraid.' The young man in the doorway misread her expression. 'I am Joseph Olungu. I am a friend of Dr Baxter.'

'Yes, I know,' Dee assured him. 'I wasn't scared. I just thought you were going to be someone else.'

'I am sorry,' he said with measured politeness. 'Perhaps I should have rung the bell.'

'Don't be silly, you live here.' Dee was the intruder, not this handsome young African. 'Baxter's gone to Edinburgh. He should be back in the evening.'

The boy nodded, perhaps already aware of this. 'I have been staying at a friend's. The doctor left message that he is home. I come quickly.'

He gave 'the doctor' capitals, his respect for Baxter Ross evident.

'I hope not that he is angry,' he concluded.

'I shouldn't think so,' Dee volunteered, although she wasn't sure if she qualified as an expert on the subject. 'I'm Dee, by the way. Perhaps Baxter's mentioned me…?'

Joseph shook his head. 'You now stay here also?'

'For a little while,' she confirmed.

'That is good,' he replied, face solemn. 'The doctor works very hard. He needs a woman in his house.'

Dee frowned, wondering what was meant by this. Clearly Joseph didn't know that she'd been lined up as *his* woman, not Baxter's.

'I have brought food for African dish—' he held up a bag of groceries '—Dr Baxter likes. You wish to cook, perhaps?'

'Not me!' Dee declared emphatically. 'I don't cook— African or otherwise.'

This drew a puzzled look from Joseph. Possibly all women cooked in his country.

'And I'm not Baxter's woman,' she added, for the record. 'He's letting me stay here because I've hurt my leg, that's all.'

'Yes, that is Baxter,' he declared in admiration. 'He is very great man. In Kirundi he is called "Le Médecin du Ciel".'

It took Dee a moment to realise it was French, not Kirundian, he was speaking, then she translated for herself.

'The Doctor from Heaven?' she said in some doubt.

'From the sky,' Joseph amended, then grinned. 'Though some think he come from heaven, too, when he arrives in helicopter... My family, we know better, of course. We are educated. My uncle was in government, and my father doctor, too,' he claimed proudly.

Snap, Dee almost said, but didn't think his English was up to such colloquialisms. French was obviously his second language—she knew Kirundi was an ex-colony of France or Belgium.

She smiled instead, then crossed to pick up the cafetière of fresh coffee she'd made.

'Want one?' she offered.

'If you please,' he agreed with Gallic formality, and sat where she placed his cup on the breakfast bar.

Dee took the seat opposite, saying, 'Would you prefer to speak French? I'm a little out of practice, but I studied it at school.'

'No, thank you.' He acknowledged the offer with another smile. 'I must practise my English in case I am permitted to study here.'

'What would you like to study?'

'Medicine.'

Dee was hardly surprised. With his father and his mentor both doctors, it seemed inevitable.

'But maybe I do not get to stay,' he concluded, grave once more.

Maybe he'd get deported, Dee added silently to herself. 'What will you do if you have to go back?'

His face clouded over. 'It is difficult. I think I will have no choice but to fight.'

Difficult wasn't the word for it. Dee listened as Joseph went on to tell her something of the civil war tearing apart what had once been a relatively prosperous African nation. No wonder Baxter wanted to keep him here.

Her own problems paled into insignificance. In fact, she began to question if she really had any. She had a roof over her head and food to eat. She had a job of sorts, too. And Baxter Ross? Well, what feeling she had for him was surely a delusion.

She reminded herself of that later, when Baxter returned to the feast Joseph had prepared with her help. Her heart might be racing like a train, her pulse in overdrive, but nerves could do that.

She watched the two men greet each other with wide smiles and a hug that might have been between father and son.

She waited for him to turn to her with a hard face that would stop the train.

Only he didn't. Last night had evidently been forgotten or forgiven. When he finally looked at her, it was with a gaze of concern.

'You okay?' he asked in quiet tones.

'Fine,' she nodded.

Fine, she lied, and stood there, eyes fixed on his beautiful face, as the train went faster and faster. She saw the crash coming, but didn't want to jump off.

It was just a delusion, so why did it seem so real, so painful, this feeling she had for him?

CHAPTER TEN

DEE sat in the bow of the boat, her fingers trailing in the water. They'd caught the breeze and were now skimming across the firth, Baxter at the tiller.

It had surprised her when he'd first asked her to join him sailing. She'd assumed he wanted solitude. He'd asked Joseph, too, but Joseph couldn't swim and hadn't been keen.

Dee hadn't been sure herself. Not scared, just concerned she would do something stupid and annoy him. She'd quickly taken to it, however, and over that summer had developed a passion for it quite separate from her desire for his company.

Whenever he asked her, it was offhand. 'I'm going out on the boat. Want to come?'

Her answer was always equally casual. 'Sure. Why not?' But her heart sang a different tune.

The tune varied. Sometimes it was a song full of bright hope as he smiled at her and laughed with her and gave every sign of liking having her around. Other times it was a sad lament, when he seemed so remote she wondered who she was kidding—only herself?

'Do you want to navigate for a while?' he asked, now catching her eyes on him.

No, she wanted to look at him. But she could hardly say so.

'Yes, okay.'

Carefully they changed positions in the boat.

She took the tiller and concentrated on steering. It was he who watched her then, and she blushed on finding his cool blue eyes on her.

But his interest was purely professional.

'Are you still taking the iron tablets Alan prescribed?' he enquired.

'Yes,' she replied shortly.

Alan was the local GP, and an old schoolfriend of Baxter's. He'd turned up on the second evening of Dee's stay to give her a check-up. He'd drained the knee again, stressing how essential it was to rest it. He'd also put her on a course of iron supplements to combat anaemia.

'You certainly look healthier,' added Baxter.

If it was a compliment, Dee didn't let it go to her head. It was so doctorish. Not prettier, sexier, more interesting—merely healthier.

'Perhaps you'll be able to stop taking the tablets soon,' he suggested.

And leave? Dee's eyes flew to his. Was that the next item on the agenda? Mend leg, raise blood count, then goodbye—was that the final goal?

Of course it was!

Baxter watched her expression cloud over. 'Something wrong?'

'No,' Dee denied. Nothing wrong. What else could she expect? Pride told her to jump before she was pushed. 'I was just thinking it's time I moved on.'

'What?' He seemed surprised.

Dee wished she could take back the words. 'I—I...'

'If it's what you want, I can't stop you.'

She'd imagined it was what *he* wanted.

'Have you somewhere in mind?' he pursued.

'Nowhere specific,' she admitted. 'A bedsit in Edinburgh, maybe.'

'With Henry in tow?' He arched a brow, suggesting she hadn't thought very hard about this. 'And what will you do for money?'

Dee shot him a resentful look, in no mood for this inquisition, then fixed her eyes ahead and, rather late, saw the cruiser cutting through the water towards them.

'Help! Which way?' She gripped the tiller hard.

'Port,' he instructed briskly, at the same time dropping the sail to kill their speed.

'Port?' She froze for a moment.

He reached over to show her, but she was already jerking the tiller across. The rest followed as inevitably as day followed night. The boom swung. He ducked. The boat rocked. He looked ready to fall. She stood to save him. They both fell.

She was under the water maybe thirty seconds before she came up, gasping for breath and grasping at the boat. She didn't have time to get scared. Baxter was there at her side, strong arm on her waist.

'You're all right. I've got you,' he assured her, and quelled any notion of panic.

She nodded and muttered through chattering teeth, 'Sorry.'

She wasn't sure exactly what had happened, but she knew it had been her fault.

'Happens,' he dismissed, then worried eyes searched her face for any sign of injury before he said, 'Let's get you out of the water.'

Dee didn't argue, but gratefully let him boost her aboard before he climbed in himself.

Then reaction set in as she watched him empty each of his deck shoes in turn, and she started to laugh.

Fortunately he saw the funny side, too, and they laughed together, regardless of their dripping hair and wet-through clothes—they would dry in the sun, anyway.

It didn't put Dee off sailing either, though it rained hard the next time they went out, and they ended up almost as wet as the time they'd fallen in.

Baxter admired her hardiness, while his sister declared them both mad.

At any rate, there was no further mention of her leaving. Perhaps the arrangement suited him, too. Cat joked that he was keeping Dee around to ward off past girlfriends who might hear he was now available on a full-time basis. It was possible. A woman had rung a few times in the first fortnight of his return, but, to Dee's knowledge, he hadn't dated anyone.

Their lives gradually fell into a pattern. Baxter drove to Edinburgh in his battered old Range Rover most week days for his research job at the university. Joseph sometimes accompanied him, and sometimes went by moped if he was to spend the evening with friends he'd made at his summer school. Dee stayed at home with Henry, cleaning to earn her keep, walking in the hills now her leg was better, and sometimes minding Morag while Cat went for her antenatal visits or into Edinburgh for shopping.

It wasn't a bad life. In fact, it was a great life compared to the one she'd had over the last couple of years. Though the tower was isolated, it was peaceful rather than lonely. She played the flute for her own enjoyment, read copiously and spent some of the time studying various prospectuses for local and city colleges.

As she had already done a year's work for A levels in English literature, French and history, it made sense to follow similar courses for the coming academic year. She was not prepared, however, to accept Baxter's offer to pay her fees for a sixth form at one of the prestigious Edinburgh schools. Money aside, she felt too old to play the role of schoolgirl any more.

The truth was she was content to live in limbo for the moment. The days went by pleasurably, and Baxter was always home by six-thirty. The evenings followed on from that. He turned out to be something of a new man—well, as far as the kitchen was concerned. He could cook, so he did, while Dee took care of the dogsbody parts, the vegetables, setting the table, washing the dishes. Joseph, when home, was excused from duties to study; he hoped to go to medical school if he achieved refugee status.

After dinner they went for a walk or played chess; they were surprisingly well-matched, Baxter and her, but Joseph could beat both of them. Or they just sat around, talking about everything and nothing.

Weekends started on Friday, when Baxter drove her to the supermarket. The first few times she had done a list, but Baxter maintained that took the pleasure out of it and they did it his way, going up and down aisles, selecting at random. Saturdays were spent sailing, as often as not, unless Morag talked Baxter into a trip to the zoo or the latest Disney film, and then he had Dee come along for moral support.

It didn't help to get over him, of course, going so many places together. It might have, if he'd been stuffy and boring, but he wasn't. He was sharp and witty, and the coolest, most laid-back person she'd ever met. He knew what was important and didn't bother with the things that weren't.

The fact was, he was her soul mate.

The trouble was, only she recognised the fact.

He never seemed to get beyond seeing her as the skinny kid with the cropped hair and the multiplicity of earrings, despite her current mass of blond waves and the subtle studs in her ears, and the filled-out figure that had *other* men noticing.

How she wished she were older! Yet, when her birthday came around, she didn't tell anyone. 'Older' wasn't eighteen, and she didn't want him reminded of the age difference.

He found out anyway, the next day. It was Saturday, and he collected the post from the doorstep, bringing it upstairs to the breakfast table. He removed the elastic band holding it together and, after throwing a couple of circulars straight into the bin, came upon a large yellow envelope.

'For you.' He handed it to Dee.

She knew what it must be from its shape, and a glance at the postmark told her who had sent it.

When she made no move to open it, he said, 'It's not your birthday, is it?'

'No, it was yesterday,' she replied in dismissive tones.

'I did not know.' Joseph gave her an apologetic look from across the table.

'Ditto.' Baxter gave her a frown.

'Happy birthday, Deborah,' Joseph added in his formal way.

'Thanks,' Dee smiled shyly.

'Yes, many happy returns,' Baxter agreed, but there was an edge to his voice. He indicated the envelope discarded by her plate. 'Aren't you going to open it?'

'Yes, all right.' She did it with some reluctance.

She drew out a stylish card with '18' on the front. The message inside wasn't exactly warm. Just 'Love, Mother'. No invitations to come home. The cheque, she supposed, was compensation.

'Your stepfather?' Baxter surmised.

She met his eyes. They reflected the disdain in his voice. He still imagined she'd had some kind of relationship with Edward.

'No, it's from my mother,' she informed him coolly. 'Along with this.'

She showed him the cheque. She felt she had to. He let her stay here because she had no money. Five hundred pounds changed that.

'That's good. I'm pleased for you,' he said, his tone warmer.

'Well, at least I'm not broke any more,' she replied with a heavy heart.

She waited to see if he would say anything. Such as, Why don't you use it to move out?

He gave her a wry look instead. 'For a week or so, anyway.'

Dee took a moment to catch his meaning. 'You think I'd go and blow it, just like that?'

'Why not?' he shrugged. 'That's what money's for—well, when you're eighteen, anyway,' he qualified. 'You can take us out to the pub tonight, celebrate your new legal drinking status.'

'Yes, okay,' Dee agreed quite readily, then realised she couldn't. 'No, I forgot. Your sister's asked me to babysit.'

He made a slight face. 'You can't let her down, I suppose.'

Dee wished she could. Going to the pub with Baxter and Joseph was hardly high living, but at least it would be something to mark her coming of age. She'd spent yesterday feeling very sorry for herself.

'I could take you tomorrow night,' she suggested.

'Fine by me,' Baxter accepted.

'And I,' Joseph said in his precise English.

'It's a date, then,' Baxter confirmed.

A date. Dee silently echoed the words, wishing it were true. But then how would she feel if he really went on a date—with someone else? It had to happen soon. Cat had said it was rare for him to go so long without female company. What if he brought her here? Slept with her upstairs…?

Dee shut her eyes on the thought. When she opened them again, it was to see Baxter's face go grim as he sorted through the rest of his mail and came to an official-looking letter.

'Home Office—the result of your appeal, I suspect.' He offered it to Joseph.

The younger man swallowed hard. 'You read it, Doctor, please.'

No birthday card, this; Dee tensed, too. She watched Baxter read and reread the typed letter with the Home Office heading. Not good news, either.

Joseph must have gathered that, too. When he next spoke, it was in some language Dee didn't recognise. She assumed it was Kirundian.

Baxter answered in the same tongue, fluent from the years he'd spent there. His face was grave. He was holding out no false hope.

Joseph was clearly struggling with some strong emotions. Rather than display them, he got up and left the room.

Dee's impulse was to follow, but Baxter laid a detaining hand on her arm. 'Joseph comes from a proud people. He won't thank you for seeing him upset.'

'Is that it?' she asked. 'The last chance he had of staying?'

A nod from Baxter confirmed it. 'They're giving him a couple of months' grace to prepare for deportation.'

Dee was a little stunned. She'd been aware of Joseph's predicament from the outset, but she'd naively believed he would keep getting reprieves.

'We have to help him,' she stated, and, knowing only one way *she* could, added, 'Dee is willing.'

Baxter slid her a hard glance, but remained silent. She wondered if he understood the literary allusion.

'It's from Dickens. "Barkis is willin'"'. It means—' she began to explain.

'I know what it means,' he cut across her, his face tight. 'I just don't find it funny.'

'It wasn't meant to be.' Dee had joked merely to cover any doubts. 'I will do it… It's why I'm here, after all.'

He stared at her briefly, but if she'd expected him to be grateful she was sadly mistaken.

'No, it isn't, not any more.' He scraped back his chair, heading for the door as he said, 'I have some calls to make, then I'm going out.'

Dee was left feeling wounded. It had been his idea that Joseph marry a British citizen, yet, when it came to the crunch, he didn't trust her to do it. Did he think she would mess it up somehow and betray them all?

Dee veered between self-pity and anger, and in the end anger won. Because he was wrong—wrong on all counts. This wasn't about how *he* felt or what he thought of her. This was about Joseph rapidly running out of options. Surely it was his choice?

It was in that mood Dee approached Joseph later, taking a sandwich up to his room. Despite everything, he'd returned to his studies. Maybe it was his mechanism for coping.

'Joseph, has Baxter ever told you why he brought me up here?' she asked him outright.

Joseph frowned as if he considered it an odd question. 'You had an injured leg.'

'Yes.' Dee tried again. 'Well, has he ever talked to you of marriage as a solution to your problem?'

'Marriage to a British citizen?' Joseph showed he understood. 'He joke about it once, but it is not possible. I know no one to marry.'

Clearly he had never regarded her as a candidate, and Dee hadn't done so herself lately. There was only one man she imagined marrying, but that was fantasy. This was reality.

She took a deep breath, before saying, 'You know me.'

Joseph looked uncertain, then decided it must be English humour, and laughed.

Dee remained unsmiling. 'I mean it.'

He still treated it with disbelief. 'You cannot marry me. Baxter would not permit, I think. You are his *chère amie*.'

Dear friend? Dee wondered what ground such a term covered in Kirundi. Lover? No, that would be *amour*.

'What makes you say that?' She forced a laugh, as if it was nonsense.

Joseph, however, wasn't so naive. 'I see you look at him. I see him look at you. Perhaps you ask him to marry you instead,' he suggested.

'What?' This time Dee didn't have to force a laugh. The idea was genuinely absurd. 'Is that what happens in Kirundi? The woman asks the man?'

'No, Kirundi is very traditional. Man asks father, gives goats.' A smile acknowledged possible flaws in such a custom. 'But in Britain girl can choose. You do not want Baxter?'

Dee wasn't expecting a question so direct, and felt her cheeks flame.

'I am sorry.' Joseph detected her embarrassment. 'I do not mean to offend.'

'You haven't,' Dee said, recovering. 'It's just not an option, Baxter and I. In fact, it was his suggestion, initially, that I marry you.'

Joseph looked amazed, then puzzled, before shaking his head. He didn't understand Europeans. He liked them, but they often made no sense to him.

'Anyway, I have no plans to marry anyone else,' she continued. 'So, if it would keep you here, I'd be willing.'

'Tu es très gentil.' Joseph lapsed into French as he applauded her kindness. *'Je ne sais…* I do not know what to say, but I must ask the doctor.'

So much for cutting out the middle man, but Dee didn't try to persuade Joseph otherwise. She supposed any marriage would need *the doctor*'s co-operation.

She told herself she didn't care what he thought, but was relieved that he was still absent when Ewan came to fetch her for babysitting. Cat had invited her to sleep at their cottage, and it suited Dee. If Joseph spoke to Baxter that night, he might have cooled down by the morning.

Cat noticed her distraction when she arrived and asked if anything was wrong, but Dee just shook her head. Cat had her own problems. Over seven months pregnant, she felt heavy and tired most of the time, and was not looking forward to a business dinner involving clients of Ewan's management consultancy.

'I look like a beached whale,' Cat declared, in her long caftan dress.

'You look beautiful.' Ewan's eyes lingered on his wife's face, telling her he meant it.

Cat glowed with pleasure even as she murmured, 'Liar.'

Dee watched with genuine fascination. They'd been married over ten years, but love had clearly not been eroded in that time. Dee didn't know anyone—her parents, her friends' parents, her parents' friends—who had a marriage this happy.

'You give me a row when I lie,' Morag pointed out as her mother bent down to kiss her.

'Don't worry, darling,' Cat laughed back. 'Daddy'll be getting his just deserts later.'

Ewan gave a fake leer at the prospect, while Morag took it quite literally and wanted to know why Daddy was getting a pudding for telling fibs.

The adults all laughed, and Cat was saved any further explanation as a taxi arrived to transport them to the country club where they were to have dinner.

Dee had babysat Morag often, and had grown to like her despite her precocious ways. They played a little Junior Monopoly before Dee took her upstairs and read her a pile of books until she finally nodded off. Then Dee went downstairs to the guest bedroom, turning in early, and willed herself to sleep rather than lie awake worrying about Baxter's reaction to her proposal to Joseph.

She woke with a start some time later, roused by persistent knocking on the front door.

Still drowsy, she padded along the corridor, calling out, 'Just coming,' as she turned the key. She'd left it in the lock, which she assumed must be why Cat and Ewan couldn't get in.

Only it wasn't Cat and Ewan—a fact she didn't realise until she opened the door and Baxter strode past her.

Once in the hallway, he let his gaze rake her from head to foot as she stood, sleepy-eyed and barely dressed, still using one of his shirts as a nightgown.

He launched an attack before she even had time to draw breath.

'Have you any idea what this is for?' He shut the door and held up the chain on it.

'Yes.'

'Have you any idea how it works?'

'Of course.'

Dee shot him a look of resentment. She wasn't stupid, and he knew it.

'But you still answered the door, half-awake and *half-naked*.' He let his gaze rest on the cleavage revealed by the loosely buttoned shirt.

Dee's hand went to her neck and pulled the sides of the shirt together. 'I thought it was Cat and Ewan.' She stated the obvious.

'I could have been anyone,' he countered, in the same tight, angry voice.

'Yeah, okay.' Dee stopped trying to defend herself. He was right. She had been careless. 'What do you want, anyway?' she asked instead.

'What do you think I want?' he threw back at her.

A fight, Dee judged by the deep scowl on his brow, but found it hard to summon up an appropriate response. It took a moment or two before she even recalled what offence she'd committed this time.

'Joseph,' she finally sighed.

'Yes, Joseph,' he grated back. 'What else?'

Dee shrugged in response, as if it could have been one of many things.

'*Is* there something else?' he added seeing her expression.

'Who knows?' she replied wearily. 'You pretty much disapprove of everything I do.'

'That's not true,' he denied, then grabbed her arm when she would have walked away from him. 'Where do you think you're going?'

'The kitchen,' she replied shortly. 'Unless you want to wake Morag with your shouting.'

'I…am…not…shouting!' He bit out each word in suppressed temper, then added, 'Right. The kitchen.'

Dee found herself being propelled in that direction, and her own temper started rising.

She put the table between them and, dry-mouthed, poured a glass of water for herself.

He helped himself too, but, in his case, it was to a glass of whisky from a bottle he took from a cupboard. He obviously knew his way round the kitchen.

He drank it down as if in need of it, then caught her eye on him. 'Do you want a glass?'

She pursed her lips. 'I don't drink spirits.'

'How abstemious.' He mocked her tone and poured another for himself. 'Or maybe you just haven't had the time to acquire a taste... What is it? Forty-eight hours since you've been legally entitled to get legless?'

'I've been drunk before.' Dee wasn't setting herself up to be holier than thou. 'I just didn't like it.'

A shadow briefly crossed her face as she remembered. That New Year's party. Tipsy on wine. Kissing that boy. Then Edward kissing her. The shock had sobered her up quickly enough. She hadn't got drunk again.

'What happened?'

'Nothing.'

Nothing apart from her life changing for ever. But Dee wasn't in the confessing mood. Nor was he in a listening mood.

'What about this afternoon? What happened then?'

'With Joseph...?'

'Yes, with Joseph,' he clipped out, impatient at her vagueness. 'Unless, of course, you proposed to more than one person today.'

'Not as I recall.' She adopted a bored air against his sarcasm, and saw the knuckles of his hand clench on his whisky glass.

But Dee wasn't scared. Not physically. She'd lived with Baxter Ross long enough to know some things. He would never hit her.

'Is this some kind of game to you?' he demanded, rapping the glass back on the work surface. 'To get at me through Joseph?'

Dee frowned. She genuinely didn't understand.

'I don't see that it's doing anything to you,' she replied. 'It's Joseph I'm marrying.'

'For the money?' he returned harshly. 'Is that it? Because if it is—'

'You can keep your money!' Dee matched his contempt.

'Then why?' He hadn't conceived that she might be moved by Joseph's plight.

'Does it matter?' she drawled. 'It's other people's perception that's important. And who's to say I haven't fallen in love with Joseph? We've been living in the same house for long enough.'

Dee felt it could be a convincing scenario.

Too convincing perhaps, because Baxter threw back, 'Are you saying you have?'

'Have what?'

'Fallen in love?'

Dee felt her cheeks go pink. Oh, she'd done that all right. Just not with Joseph.

'No, of course not.' She hid behind scorn. 'I told you— I don't believe in that crap.'

He grimaced at her language, before saying, 'So why would you be doing it, if not for the money?'

'Use your imagination,' Dee suggested.

The point was, she'd used hers and she still couldn't see it—Joseph, with a Kalashnikov in his hands, and dead eyes like the other young men in the newsreels he and Baxter compulsively watched. She refused to see it.

'It was your idea, remember?' she added.

His face darkened. 'I didn't know you then.'

'And, now you do,' she concluded, 'you don't trust me to carry it off. Well, fine! Great! Let Joseph get his head blown off rather than risk it.'

Dee meant it as her final word, and stalked towards the door.

He intercepted her, a hand pulling her round. 'It isn't a matter of trust, dammit!'

'Oh, right! Yes! So what is it?'

'Don't you know?'

His eyes burned into hers, accusing her of something.

Dee's defence was her frown. She really hadn't a clue what he meant.

'You don't, do you?' he concluded for himself, anger cooling even as he stated, 'You can't marry Joseph.'

'Okay, find someone else for him.' She countered what seemed a purely arbitrary decision. 'Maybe one of your ex-girlfriends would do it.'

His sighed heavily. 'Don't be absurd.'

'Of course, I forgot,' she flipped back. 'They're all too bloody old for Joseph!'

He'd offended her—it seemed fair to return the compliment.

'Being my age, you mean?'

'Whatever.'

'Thirty-four—you really think that's so old?'

Dee wished she hadn't started this. Who would have thought he'd be so sensitive?

'It was a joke,' she pouted, and tried to pull away.

He wouldn't let her. 'But you think it all the same, right?'

'No, you're the one who thinks it.' Dee was tired of being on the defensive. 'You're the one who bangs on about the age difference and acts like you're my damned father!'

His expression went from stiff to rigid. She'd gone too far.

'On the contrary,' he ground out, 'I'd say I *haven't* acted like your father—or more precisely your stepfather... Maybe that's my mistake.'

Dee's eyes blazed at mention of Edward, and she might have struck Baxter if he hadn't grabbed her arms.

'Is that what you want?' He dragged her body against his and she realised in shock that he was already aroused. 'Is this what you like? To know your power over men?'

Her own response was immediate and alarming, but it was all wrong—to feel desire in such circumstances. 'No, please...'

'"No, please",' he mocked her. 'How virginal! But are you? I wonder...'

Anger returned, overshadowing any love Dee had for him.

'That's for me to know—' she hissed at him, recklessly, foolishly.

'And presumably for me to find out?' he finished with a smile that didn't reach his eyes. 'Is that an invitation?'

'No, it bloody well isn't!' Dee pushed at the wall of his chest. 'Let me go!'

'Not yet.' She continued struggling, and he backed her hard against the door. 'You started this game of dare, so why not finish it? You want to be treated like a woman, don't you?'

Dee didn't know what she wanted any more. She went still as a hand was placed on her neck, tilting her head upwards. She stared back at him in defiance, but refused to turn away as he lowered his mouth to hers.

He kissed her without passion, meaning to punish.

She clenched her lips, meaning to resist.

But it was hard. It was so long since they'd been this close, so long since he'd held her, and somehow the anger got lost and the kiss became something else—a soft, persuasive murmur on her lips, a call to the senses, sweet and clear, until she began kissing him back, her body swaying to his.

When he finally raised his head, she couldn't remember why they'd been arguing. She just stood there, transfixed by longing, wide blue eyes willing him to kiss her again.

'This isn't right.' The words were a whisper, fading away even as he cupped her face in his hands, even as his mouth sought hers once more.

Lips touched, then parted. Breath caught, then quickened. Desire stirred, then flared.

They weren't playing games any more, and Dee didn't hide how she felt, snaking her arms round his neck, her mouth opening to his, accepting his passion, giving him her love. She felt excited rather than alarmed as he began to kiss her deeply, demanding more. Closer he drew her, and she went, wrapping her body round his, until he acknowledged his need for her with a groan. Then it was hands touching through clothes—restless, seeking, urgent—their mouths kissing, hard and hungry, breathless with desire.

'Not here,' Dee managed to gasp when he would have pulled her down onto the floor.

'No, not here,' Baxter echoed as he remembered where they were, and grabbed her hand.

He pulled her with him out into the hallway and along the darkened corridor to the spare room.

With some last vestige of sanity, Dee tried to say something about Morag being upstairs and Cat not liking it. But he started to kiss her again, hands sliding down to the soft curve of her hips and lifting her body to the heat of his.

Then his mouth left hers to follow the long arch of her throat, touching the wildly beating pulse, tasting her sweet-smelling skin down the hollow at her throat until he reached the barrier of her clothing. Frustrated by it, he backed her towards the high brass bed, undoing the buttons of her shirt as they went. With each button that was undone his lips touched the exposed skin, trailing down the valley between her breasts until the sides of the shirt parted.

Dee was left trembling. She stood before him, wanting more yet dreading it, too. He raised his head, and for a moment his eyes searched her face. She hid her love, knowing he didn't want it. She hid her fear, too, as he slipped the shirt down her arms, letting it fall to the floor. She was naked yet it was her face he continued to watch, his eyes holding hers, keeping her there, a willing captive, as he stripped off his own shirt to reveal a broad chest matted by dark hair.

When Baxter finally moved his gaze downwards, it was to find the reality of her was better even than his memory— the swollen pout of her mouth, the long, graceful neck, the tanned slope of her shoulders merging with the paleness of milk, a woman's breasts, proud and full, over a narrow ribcage and flat stomach, skin smooth as silk until the tri-angle of hair between her thighs, then smooth again on her endless legs.

His eyes caressed each part of her as he made love to her in his mind. Dee might have felt shame, but didn't. His gaze told her more clearly than words that he thought her beautiful.

It was when he finally touched her, smoothing a hand down her arm, that she shivered.

'You're cold.'

She let him believe it, and he drew her into his arms, offering her his warmth. But the shock of it, his hard, hair-covered body against the soft contours of hers, made her shiver more, and he led her to the bed.

'Lie down.' She did as he said, and he covered her with the sheet.

Still shivering, Dee watched as he finished undressing himself. He unstrapped his watch first, placing it on the bedside table, before unbuckling his belt. He stripped off his jeans, socks and shoes, leaving on his boxer shorts as he climbed into the bed with her.

The heat of the moment had gone, but it didn't seem to matter. He still wanted her. The hand that touched her hair, her cheek, her lips, told her that. And Dee realised she'd been waiting for this ever since her first night at the tower. She felt nerves, not fear. She loved this man.

'I'm afraid I have nothing.' He brushed a lock of hair from her face. 'So this time's for you.'

Dee was slow to realise what he meant. No protection. She hadn't even thought about it.

She should have been grateful to him, but it told her how used he was to this situation. She was one of many. She had to remember that.

'Don't worry.' He misunderstood her frown. 'If you don't like anything, just say... Okay?'

'Okay.' Dee wondered if it was too late to say stop.

He gazed across the pillow at her, and the idea drifted away. When he softly demanded, 'Kiss me,' she didn't hesitate.

She leaned over him and he lay back on the pillow, his hand lightly caressing the nape of her neck. She lowered her head to his and he lay passive for a moment, perhaps needing a sign of her willingness. He got it in the sweet touch of her lips moving on his, and he didn't wait for more.

He caught Dee by surprise as he slid an arm down her bare back, holding her body to his, while the other hand was in her hair, cradling her head as he stole her breath and her reason with a kiss so intimate it left her shaking.

He was still kissing her when he rolled her over until she was on her back and he was above her, then his mouth moved elsewhere—everywhere—her face, her cheek, her hair, then trailed downwards to her neck, her shoulders, his lips leaving their imprint, gently biting, licking the light sweat on her skin, tasting her, tormenting her till she could bear it no longer and, her fingers entwined in his hair, put her breast to the mouth that sought it.

He took it with a groan of pleasure and made sweet, agonising circles with his tongue until she ached for the roughly sensual bite and play of his teeth and mouth. She moaned, unable to stop, as he sucked on one breast and touched the other, making longing turn to pain and spreading its sweet agony through her body.

He knew, knew it all—how to touch her, where, when. She was gasping by the time he slid his hand to her belly, where desire furled and unfurled like a living thing at the core of her being. She was ready yet not ready, recoiling instinctively when he finally touched her between the silk of her thighs.

He kissed her mouth again, her throat, her breasts, until she opened for him and the slow, pleasuring stroke of his fingers, and moaned aloud at each wave that was rising and falling, flowing through her, washing over her, higher and higher till she cried aloud in final understanding of his words—*this time's for you…this time's for you!*

She opened her eyes wide in that moment and met his. She felt that her face was bare, all emotion exposed, but she could do nothing to cover it. She lay there catching her breath while he lay beside her, watching, knowing, his hand now a tender caress on her arm.

There was tenderness in his voice, too, as he finally murmured, 'I didn't hurt you?'

'No,' she choked out.

'Good.' He smiled briefly, before saying in more serious tones, 'You were…are a virgin, aren't you?'

Dee nodded. She supposed it must have been obvious.

'Does it matter?' Her tone implied it didn't matter to her. She wanted him to be the first…wanted him to be the last.

'It seemed wrong, with you so much younger, but now…' He shook his head as if everything had changed. 'I don't know any more. I'm not sure what you want from me.'

His love. That was all. That was everything.

But Dee was no fool. She knew how the game was played.

'Isn't this enough?' She smiled as if it were for her.

He looked uncertain. Perhaps he couldn't believe his luck—a woman who didn't try to tie him down.

Dee felt she had to convince him. She slid her arms round his neck once more and pulled his mouth down to hers. If he hesitated, it was only briefly. The next moment he was kissing her with an intimacy that told her desire hadn't faded for him—or for her—and that all idea of restraint was fast disappearing.

Later Dee acknowledged she would have done anything for him—anything he asked, anything he wanted, regardless.

Only time ran out for them with the sound of a car crunching into the driveway.

They broke off their lovemaking and raised their heads.

Panic crossed Dee's face as she realised who it had to be. She looked up at Baxter's face, expecting her feelings to be reflected there.

He merely grimaced. 'Don't worry, it'll just be Cat.'

'*Just Cat!*' she cried back, already scrambling from underneath him.

He let her go, laughing dryly, 'Cat's well aware I sleep with women.'

He seemed amused by the situation, but Dee wasn't.

'It's not *your* reputation that bothers me,' she retorted as, modesty forgotten, she dived across the bed for her shirt.

Baxter remained cool, leaning back to admire the view. 'You have a birthmark.'

Dee knew she had a birthmark—knew where, too. She jumped off the bed, dragging the quilt round her to hide it.

She didn't think of the consequences until she turned to discover him, quiltless, and making no effort to cover himself. An image of long limbs and a flat, muscular torso imprinted itself in her brain before she swerved her eyes upwards to his face.

'Please.' She couldn't bear to have Cat think she was easy—even if she was!

Her distress registered, and Baxter finally rose to pull on his jeans and shirt. He did so calmly, slipping, sockless, into his shoes while a desperate Dee searched for her nightshirt. He found that first, too, and helped her into it, bending to kiss her mouth as he did so.

Dee's heart stopped for a moment. It was a deeply sensual kiss. Even with his sister at the door and sanity returned, he still wanted her.

Dee hadn't time to sort it out in her head as they heard Cat and Ewan entering the hall, then calling their names. Of course; they would have seen Baxter's car outside.

'Make the bed,' he instructed. 'And if they come in here leave the talking to me.'

Dee did as she was told, desperately straightening the cover and pillows.

She was aware of him opening a window, and for a second she thought he was going to climb out of it. But he remained where he was, calling out, 'In here, Sis,' as footsteps approached the door.

Cat entered, then stopped dead in the doorway, eyes going from Dee, combing desperate fingers through a mess of hair, to her brother, casually standing by the window.

Dee greeted her with a smile so fixed it was painful.

Baxter was a shade more natural as he drawled, 'Dee's feeling hot. The window was jammed.'

'Right.' Cat Macdonald's eyes rested on a dishevelled Dee before switching past her to the bedside table.

Dee followed her gaze to find Baxter's wristwatch still where he'd left it under the lamp.

Then Cat's attention returned to Baxter, noting the sweat on his brow with a dry, 'You seem to be suffering from the heat as well... Perhaps you need a cold shower.'

Cat's tongue was firmly in her cheek as she traded looks with her brother.

'Good idea.' He greeted the suggestion with a smile. 'I'll be off... Unless, of course, Dee wants to come home now?' His eyes fixed on Dee, clearly asking her to go back to the tower with him.

She knew if she did they would continue what they'd started, but then what? Carry on acting as normal? Get up the next day and pretend nothing had happened? She couldn't do that.

She stood there, biting her lip, wanting to go, wanting to stay.

Cat sensed her indecision, and said, 'That's silly. Dee isn't even dressed...in case you hadn't noticed.'

'Oh, I noticed.' Baxter deflected any censure with a smile.

'Yes, and I wasn't born yesterday,' his sister countered, her tone wry.

Dee alone seemed bothered by the look of the thing. Maybe brother and sister were used to such situations. Maybe Baxter Ross had seduced half the countryside under Cat's indulgent eye.

'Odd you should say that,' Baxter ran on, 'but Dee *was*.'

'Was what?'

'Born yesterday.'

'Really?' Cat's eyes moved back to Dee. 'You should have said. Which one was it again?'

'My eighteenth,' Dee relayed.

'Eighteenth?' Cat repeated, as if it was a surprise to her, then arched a brow in Baxter's direction.

His lips quirked slightly. 'All right, I know. I don't need the lecture.'

'I wasn't going to give one,' his sister denied. 'I just hope you've thought about what you're doing.'

'I have, believe me,' Baxter confirmed dryly.

Dee realised her age was the issue, and resented the two-way discussion that excluded her. Did Baxter still think she was a child?

He tried a slanting smile on her and she blanked him.

'Well, congratulations.' Cat reverted to a lighter tone. 'Eighteen. It's the big one these days. We should mark it.'

'I'm going to,' Dee returned. 'I'll send you an invitation.'

'Invitation? You're having a party?' Cat enquired.

Dee shook her head. 'Wedding. I'm getting married.'

'Getting married?' Cat echoed with a gasp, then veered between shock and apparent delight. 'You mean…? I don't believe it! Baxter, why didn't you say something? How fantastic!'

Baxter didn't answer. His gaze was intent on Dee; she had certainly wiped the smile off his face. She knew then there would be no future for her with this man.

Dee let him sweat a moment longer before she added, 'To Joseph.'

'Joseph?' Cat echoed. 'But I thought…'

It was obvious what she'd thought. Perhaps Baxter had thought it, too—that Dee was mad enough to believe marriage was on the agenda.

He looked furious, but then they *were* back where they'd started, before he'd tried to seduce her into changing her mind.

'Is this true?' Cat enquired of him, now totally bewildered.

'Ask her.' Dark blue eyes bored into Dee's.

'Yes, it is.' Dee held his gaze.

'I don't understand this.' Cat was still trying to read signals, feeling she'd misread them earlier. 'You're going to marry Joseph… Because of the immigration thing?'

Dee nodded.

'And that's all?' Cat added.

'Who knows with her?' Baxter's mouth had gone into a thin, contemptuous line.

'You approve?' His sister queried of him.

'Does it matter?' His expression said he'd had enough.

He pushed himself away from the wall and crossed to the door.

Dee's voice stopped him in his tracks. 'Yes, it does. Joseph will only do it on your say-so, and you know that.'

He rounded on her in fury. 'So what do you want from me? My blessing? God, you know how to twist the knife.'

He took a threatening step towards her, and his sister interceded, 'Please, both of you, this is crazy!'

But Baxter barely listened. 'All right, you have it,' he growled at Dee. 'My blessing... In fact, why don't you go the whole hog and ask me to give you away?'

It was pride talking. That was all. Masked his pain.

The same kind of pride governed her reply.

'How could you?' she retorted scathingly. 'I was never yours in the first place.'

'*Dee!* Stop it, please,' Cat appealed. 'Stop it before it goes too far!'

But it had already. Dee saw that. There was no going back now.

What Baxter might have said or done without his sister there was anyone's guess, but Cat's anguish finally got through to him.

With a last scornful look at Dee, he released his rage by slamming the door on his way out.

'*Baxter!*' Cat called after him, but he chose not to hear, and by the time she'd followed him out he was in his Range Rover and reversing down the drive.

'What's going on?' Ewan appeared at the corner of the stairwell.

'Not sure,' Cat admitted. 'Is Morag okay?'

'Fast asleep,' Ewan confirmed. 'I thought Dee was staying over tonight.'

'She is.'

'Then why was Baxter here?'

'Good question.' Cat frowned over the possible answers, before saying, 'You go to bed. I'll be up in a moment.'

'Well, not too long,' Ewan advised. 'Remember, we came home early because you were exhausted.'

'Yes, I know,' Cat conceded. 'But I want a word with Dee—find out just what *is* going on.'

'Mmm.' Ewan's expression told her to leave well alone.

But Cat was already walking through the cottage to the back bedroom.

She heard the sound before she even reached the room,

and any idea of interrogating Dee disappeared. How could she, when the girl was sobbing her heart out?

She knocked and called out, and the crying stopped for a moment.

It was stifled in a pillow as Dee lay, face down, silently praying for Cat to go away. She couldn't talk to her. Not his sister. For what could she say? *I'm crying because I made your brother hate me and I did that because he's breaking my heart?*

What sense did that make? What sense did any of it make?

CHAPTER ELEVEN

'How do I look?' Dee struck a pose as she emerged from the changing room.

Cat did a double take at the girl normally in jeans and sweatshirt.

It was a beautiful dress—white satin sweeping to the floor, narrowed at the waist, sleeves tight to the wrist but slipping off the shoulder to make a continuous neckline at the rise of her breasts.

It was the girl inside it, however, that made it special. She had changed from a waif with spiky hair and a match-stick body to a creature with a mass of blonde waves, a bewitching face and a figure to die for. Cat wondered when that had happened.

'Stunning,' she breathed in awe rather than envy.

Dee didn't notice as she tried to adjust the neckline so it revealed less. 'Not quite my taste, but it should do.'

'Are you sure about all this?' Cat tried once more to bring some sanity to the whole affair. 'I don't think Baxter intended you to get an actual wedding dress.'

'Didn't he?' Dee echoed indifferently.

'"Something appropriate" were the words he used to me,' Cat relayed.

And to Dee, when she'd last met him outside the minister's house.

'I'd say this fits the description.' She practised a wide, careless smile to go with the dress.

It slipped as she caught Cat's knowing expression in the mirror.

'Eat your heart out, brother dear,' the older woman murmured dryly. 'That is the point, isn't it?'

Dee pulled a face. She had avoided any discussion of her feelings over the last month—no mean feat, considering she was now live-in nanny at the Macdonalds'.

'Well, if it is, I'll be wasting my time,' Dee responded at length. 'I doubt he'll be there.'

'I wouldn't be too sure,' Cat observed. 'My brother has always had something of the masochist in his make-up. And how better to indulge it than watch the girl you want marry someone else?'

'It's not like that,' Dee denied. 'He doesn't... Well, not on a permanent basis.'

'Are you certain?' Cat asked.

'Quite.' Dee gave a firm nod. 'He thinks I'm too young for him.'

'Or he's too old?'

'Same thing.'

'It's not, actually,' Cat replied after some consideration.

But Dee had already had enough of true confessions. She said, 'I'm going to take this off,' and slipped back into the changing room.

She reckoned without a persistent Cat musing through the curtain, 'I mean, wouldn't it be awful if the only thing keeping you apart was this stupid business of age?'

'It isn't,' Dee stated briefly, stepping out of the dress and returning it to the hanger.

Cat didn't seem to hear her. 'I was rather taken aback myself the night I found the two of you together,' she ran on. 'But I've had the chance to think about it since... I was twenty-three when I met Ewan, and he was forty-one. That's an even bigger age gap than between you and Baxter, and our marriage worked.'

'It's not just age.' Dee wondered why Cat was pursuing this. She surely knew her brother wasn't really serious about her?

'Then what?' Cat asked as Dee came out again.

'I'm not his type,' Dee shrugged.

Cat snorted dismissively. 'My brother doesn't have a type. If he did, he might be settled by now... So who knows? Maybe you're it!'

Or maybe Cat wanted her to be it, Dee surmised from the word 'settled'. Perhaps his sister was scared that he would take off back to Africa, regardless of his health, unless there was something to keep him here.

'Cat,' Dee said quietly, 'I'm sure you mean well, but I'm sorry—whatever happens, I'm marrying Joseph next Saturday.'

'All right, you've made a commitment. I accept that, and if it's the only thing to save Joseph...' Cat sighed. 'It just seems so drastic, especially marrying in the church.'

'That wasn't my idea.' Dee wasn't altogether comfortable with that aspect, either.

It was Baxter who had deemed it necessary. Dee had heard it second-hand through Cat: if Dee insisted playing the martyr, she might as well do it while God was watching! It would also be more convincing to the immigration authorities.

So here they were, hiring a wedding dress and waiting for the banns to be read a third time by a local minister who had smiled favourably on the union.

That had been the worst part—deceiving the kindly old gentleman when they'd gone for the mandatory talk, pretending to be a couple, promising things that were a lie.

She'd come out of the manse house shaken, and had immediately lit up a cigarette. Joseph had been subdued, too.

'Anything wrong?' Baxter had asked, climbing down from his Range Rover where he'd been waiting outside.

It was Joseph who answered for them both. 'It is not easy, Dr Baxter, lying to a holy man. I think God will be angry.'

Baxter's lips quirked downwards, and Dee half expected him to dismiss this as rubbish. Though his parents had been missionaries, he had never exhibited the slightest sign of being religious himself.

It surprised her when he said, 'God will forgive; he sees what's in your heart,' in assurance to Joseph.

The young African seemed to take some comfort from this notion, and managed a farewell smile to Dee as Baxter opened the passenger door for him.

But when it was just Dee and Baxter, the latter certainly didn't waste any words salving *her* conscience.

Instead he muttered, 'If *you're* thinking of pulling out, say so now.'

'Why should I? It's just a load of mumbo jumbo as far as I'm concerned,' she dismissed.

He gave her a hard glance, as if testing her true feelings, and Dee stared right back at him.

Mistake. Had she really imagined she'd recovered?

She looked away, heart beating like a drum, and dragged on her cigarette.

'You're smoking again,' he remarked.

'Well spotted,' she bit back, rather than defend herself.

She'd stopped after a couple of days at the tower, but then lapsed when she'd moved to Cat's and found herself living a hundred yards from a newsagent's.

'I'm surprised Cat tolerates it,' he added, 'especially in her current condition.'

Did he have to be so pompous? 'I don't smoke in the house… Anyway, if the lecture's over, there's Ewan.'

He followed her gaze and saw his brother-in-law parking up ahead, but when she would have walked away he caught her arm. 'Not yet. You'll need this.'

He held out a cheque. It was made out to her, for six hundred pounds.

'If this is meant as a down payment for marrying Joseph—' she began angrily.

'It isn't,' he told her shortly. 'You'll have to buy something appropriate to wear for the wedding.'

'Right.' She didn't thank him. She couldn't. She just took the money and ran.

Dee fixed her mind back in the present and asked the owner of the bridal boutique, 'How much is this one to hire?'

The lady, who had been keeping at a discreet distance, beamed in satisfaction.

'Four hundred and fifty pounds for the day, plus a refundable bond of £one hundred to pay—and may I say I've never seen anyone look quite so beautiful in it?'

Dee smiled briefly, wondering how many starry-eyed brides had heard that from her.

'Fine. I'll take it.'

'When for?'

'Saturday.'

The woman's eyes widened. 'Next Saturday?'

Dee nodded. It already was *this* Saturday.

'We normally have a couple of months' notice…' The woman turned the pages of her order book 'But, yes, you're in luck. There's not many girls that can carry such a dress. It originally belonged to a model…quite famous, actually,' she confided.

'Really?' Dee made a show of being impressed, but her heart wasn't in it.

Cat paid with her credit card, having agreed to cash Baxter's cheque for Dee, and the woman let them take the dress with them rather than come back again.

'Thanks for coming with me,' Dee said to Cat over coffee in Jenner's, where they'd arranged to meet Ewan and Morag.

'Well, I would say "my pleasure",' Cat replied, 'because I love weddings. But I just wish it was for real.'

She looked genuinely gloomy, and Dee asked, 'Is it the legal aspect? Because if that's a problem for you maybe Baxter could find other witnesses.'

'No, we'll do it. The less people involved, the better,' Cat reasoned, then smiled as Morag appeared, skipping ahead of her father.

Morag was hugely excited at the prospect of a wedding, and nagged Dee mercilessly when they were in the car until Dee agreed to model the dress the moment they arrived home.

Only, when they did, it was to find Baxter leaning against the bonnet of his car.

Morag was out of the car and in his arms the second they came to a halt. Ewan and Cat also greeted him with enthusiasm.

Dee was alone in hanging back. Having looked once, and discovered her heart still doing acrobatics at the sight of him, she was careful not to look again.

She trailed the others inside, meaning to escape to her room, but Morag grabbed her hand when she tried to slip away.

Baxter also stopped her, saying, 'I have to speak to you.'

'Oh, not now.' Morag was crestfallen. 'Please Uncle

Baxie. Me and Dee are going to put on our dresses for the wedding. We'll show them to you if you like,' she added, as if that would be persuasion enough.

Uncle Baxie confined himself to a dry, 'Isn't that unlucky or something?' rather than puncture his niece's confidence.

'Only if you're the groom, brother dear,' Cat put in, careless of the hard stare she got in reply.

Morag took it as approval. 'Come on, Dee, Mum says it's all right. We'll get yours from the car…' She pulled at Dee's hand.

'All right.' Dee went rather than remain under Baxter's gaze.

By the time they fetched the dress, the others had gone through to the lounge. Whatever Baxter wanted to tell her, it could obviously keep.

She let Morag drag her upstairs to dress.

'Oh, it shines!' Morag gave her approval as she danced round Dee and the satin dress. 'Mummy said it wouldn't be a real one, but she was wrong.'

Dee wished now that it weren't. She caught sight of herself in the wardrobe mirror. The dress was still beautiful. It was she who tainted the image. She might have the right to marry in white, but it was still hypocritical. She was marrying one man while loving another.

'You'll have to brush your hair.' Morag handed her her own child's hairbrush and watched Dee do it at the dressing table before saying, 'Right, let's go downstairs. I can't wait to show Uncle Baxie.'

Dee could. She sat where she was. 'You go down,' she told the girl. 'It's you he wants to see. He won't care about seeing me.'

She smiled to make the words sound light-hearted, and perhaps she managed because Morag hesitated only briefly before taking off downstairs by herself.

Dee stayed where she was, supporting her head with an elbow, almost glaring at herself in the mirror.

What a fool she would look walking down an aisle in this dress! She just couldn't do it. She would marry Joseph, but in something simple that wouldn't underline the farce of it.

'Dee—' Morag returned at a run '—Uncle Baxie says I'm the most beautiful girl in the world, but Mum says if he thinks that he should see you, so he's coming up…'

Dee didn't hear the rest. She stood and turned just as a figure appeared in the open doorway. He came no further. He didn't need to. He had a perfect view from where he was.

His eyes went from the top of her head down to the satin shoes on her feet and back again, stopping *en route* at the rise of her breasts. He said nothing. His expression said it all. He hated it.

'It's beautiful, isn't it?' Morag pressed at his silence.

'The dress, yes,' he finally murmured.

Not the girl in it. His eyes told Dee that as they raked her once more. What other reaction could she have expected?

'I need to speak to you.' He repeated what he'd said earlier. 'Change first, and we'll go somewhere.'

His tone was impassive, so as not to distress Morag, but it still cut through Dee like a knife. They'd never really been lovers, but at least they'd once been friends. Even that was gone. There was no going back.

'He didn't really like it, did he?' Morag was astute for a five-year-old.

Dee shook her head. 'It doesn't matter. It's Joseph I'm marrying,' she reminded them both.

Morag nodded, then ventured, 'Maybe Uncle Baxie would have liked it if it was him.'

Dee wasn't sure what to reply to this, so didn't bother.

She changed back into her jeans and T-shirt and put the dress on the hanger, then covered it in Cellophane. It was the last time she would wear it, even if it was a waste of £450.

She took it down to her room on the ground floor while Morag skipped off to find the others. She hung it up in her wardrobe, then slipped out to see Henry.

The old dog had moved to the Macdonalds' with her, but Morag had turned out to be allergic to dog hair, so

they'd made him a home in the garden shed with old blan-
kets, and an oil heater for the night time.

Henry greeted her with a tail wag, but otherwise didn't
get up.

'How is he?' A voice behind her asked.

She turned to find Baxter there.

Henry wagged his tail in recognition of Baxter too, and
Baxter knelt on his haunches to pat him.

'He still manages his walk,' Dee relayed, 'but otherwise
he doesn't stray far.'

'Aye, well…he's an old dog,' Baxter warned in his gen-
tle Scots accent.

Dee understood. Her beloved Henry was growing tired,
and she might lose him soon. The thought upset her too
much to dwell on.

'What do you want?' she said instead to Baxter.

'We have to talk, but not here… Joseph's waiting back
at the tower for us.' His manner was impersonal but serious.

Dee decided not to argue. She put a handful of dog bis-
cuits down for Henry, then followed Baxter out to his car.

He drove in silence and she sat, remote from him, un-
consciously drumming her fingers on the door.

They were almost at the tower when he sighed. 'If you
really need to, you can smoke.'

She glanced at him in surprise before replying, 'I've run
out of cigarettes.'

It was actually a lie. She'd given up again, but didn't
want him to think his disapproval had been the moving
force. Morag's sniffing and asking her point-blank why she
sometimes smelled 'yuk' had proved a much better deter-
rent.

She craved one now, however, as they lapsed back into
strained silence until they reached the tower. Outside it was
parked a minicab with a waiting driver.

Baxter showed no surprise at it and made no comment.

Dee had to ask, 'Who's that for?'

'Joseph.'

'Where's he going?'

'The airport.'

'Airport?' Dee echoed in alarm. 'He's returning to Kirundi?'

'No, actually, he's not.' The denial was emphatic 'But I thought you might jump to that conclusion, so I want you to hear what's happening from his own lips.'

Dee frowned, still in the dark, but guessed enough to say, 'I take it I won't be needing any wedding dress?'

'Not to marry Joseph, no,' he confirmed. And, at her silence, prompted, 'Disappointed?'

'There was nothing going on between Joseph and I,' she stated impatiently, 'and you know it.'

'Perhaps,' he conceded, before climbing out of the car.

Dee followed, looking up at the tower. It had been weeks since she'd been here, and absence had made the heart grow fonder. It now seemed magnificent rather than bleak.

They went upstairs and met Joseph on the first landing. Another African man, dressed in suit and tie, was holding his bags.

'Deborah, I am so glad you could come,' Joseph said, smiling. 'I did not want to leave without saying goodbye. Dr Baxter has told you I am going?'

Dee nodded. 'Not where, though.'

Joseph looked towards his companion, and the man shook his head, saying something in their own language.

'I am sorry, but can only tell you a little,' Joseph ran on. 'You see, I go to join my uncle in country where he has gained political asylum.'

'The uncle who was a minister in your government?' Dee concluded.

Joseph smiled. 'Yes, my uncle Patrice. He went into hiding when it was overthrown. I did not know where until the Doctor found out. My uncle has been looking for me also, and has sent Marcelle to collect me.'

'I'm pleased for you.' Dee smiled at Joseph's evident happiness at rediscovering his family.

'Now you do not have to marry me,' he added. 'But I will always be most grateful. I give you something.' He handed her a rectangular box.

Dee took from it an oval ring set with a blue jewel so exquisite she didn't have to feign delight.

'It's beautiful.' She reached up and planted a kiss on his cheek. 'I'll keep it for ever.'

Joseph smiled, satisfied by her pleasure at his gift, then turned to take his leave of Baxter.

'There are so many things I wish to say, Doctor,' he began, but his voice was already choked.

'No need, man. No need,' Baxter dismissed, and embraced Joseph in a father-son way. 'I'll see you down.'

Too full of emotion to speak, Joseph nodded goodbye to Dee, and the men began to go downstairs with the luggage.

Dee did not follow them. She felt she would be intruding. Though she'd been only a week away from marrying Joseph, they had never been more than friends. It was Baxter who'd been important to him, Baxter who had been his hero.

He was no hero to Dee. No friend, either, considering how he'd acted.

She went through to the kitchen to wait for him, and found the place an untidy mess. Opened letters and magazines lay on work surfaces, jackets were on the backs of chairs and dirty dishes were in the sink. She stacked them at the side, then began to run the hot water before she realised what she was doing and asked herself why she was doing it. She was no longer paid to clean up after Baxter.

She didn't hide her disgust when he reappeared.

'Yeah, okay, it's in a state.' He pushed a distracted hand through his hair. 'I haven't bothered much since you've gone.'

'You didn't bother much when I was here,' Dee retorted. 'You need a cleaner.'

'Cat said she'd advertise.'

'Don't you think Cat has enough to do?'

He raised a brow at her sharp tone. 'She offered,' he told her. 'But, yes, you're probably right.'

Dee didn't want him agreeing with her. She was too cross.

'So how long has it been arranged, Joseph going to join his uncle?' She asked the question that really mattered.

'Contact was established a couple of weeks ago,' he admitted, 'but it's only in the last few days that Joseph was given official permission to enter France.'

'France?' Dee echoed. 'Why are you telling me? I thought it was hush-hush.'

'I don't want you thinking he's going somewhere dangerous,' he explained. 'And, besides, if *I* can find his uncle, I'm sure his enemies are well aware of his whereabouts too.'

'So why didn't you tell me what you were planning?' she said through clenched teeth. 'Why not tell me weeks ago I didn't have to marry him?'

'I wanted to wait till everything was cut and dried... Anyway, you never *had* to marry Joseph. You chose to,' he corrected pedantically.

'You're the one who wanted me to do it in the first place,' she accused in return.

'That was before.'

'Before what? Before you decided I wasn't reliable?'

He shook his head, and said simply, 'Before you and I.'

It stopped Dee in her tracks for a moment. The words, *There is no you and I,* rose on her lips, but the blue eyes that met hers told her she was a liar before she could speak them.

'Did you really think I'd let you marry him?' He held her gaze as he took a step towards her.

'I...' Dee didn't know what to think. 'You gave me money for the dress.'

'I wanted to see how far you'd go.' His eyes darkened. 'I saw this afternoon... What was the idea? To show me what I was missing?'

Dee remained silent, but a blush betrayed her.

'There was no need, of course.' He took another step until they were all but touching. 'I already knew what I was missing, remember?'

From the night he'd turned up at Cat's. Dee remembered too well. All of it. That had also started as an argument.

How easily one passion became another. She'd felt almost violent towards him a moment ago, and now here she was, trembling like a leaf because he was close enough to fan her cheek with his breath. Such weakness was frightening.

She hid her feelings behind an imperious, 'I'd like to go home now.'

He countered with a simple, 'You are home,' that confused her more.

Home? Here? What was he saying?

He made it clearer. 'I need you with me, Dee.'

A hand lifted to touch her face with a gentleness that touched her soul.

She shut her eyes against its warmth. 'Don't do this.'

'Why not? You want me, too.' It was a truth too obvious to deny.

'And that's enough?'

'No, but I'll settle for it.'

Dee didn't understand his answer, but then he hadn't understood the question. And in the end what did it matter? It was as inevitable as night and day, their being together.

Why else did she let him take her face in his hands and kiss her slow and hard, stealing the breath from her body, the reason from her mind? Why else did she go with him, without another word, up the spiral staircase? Why else did she accept the little on offer even as her heart was breaking with each step, crying out for more?

He took her to the room where she'd once slept, and led her towards the four-poster bed. Evening was drawing in and casting shadows across the counterpane. They didn't bother with lights, didn't bother with words.

He undressed her with almost detached efficiency and, having no will of her own, she let him. He pulled her jersey over her head, followed by her T-shirt, before bending to slip off her sneakers. Then he unzipped her jeans and slid them down her hips until she was forced to step out of them, leaving herself in a white lace bra and panties.

Dee felt chilled—not by the coolness of the room, but by his apparent lack of emotion. She watched him strip off his shirt and unbuckle his belt, and she began to move away from him. She didn't get very far, because he reached out to catch her hand and pull her towards him, turning her so her back was against his chest. Then he circled her with his strong, hair-roughened arms and drew her to his body, bending to touch the nape of her neck with his lips.

He kissed the soft hollow at her throat, the leap of her pulse, and Dee's head fell back as a wave of desire went through her. It spread with his hands as they reached up to cup a breast, down to splay over her taut stomach. It became a flood as he slid his way past the barrier of her clothing to touch her in places only he knew.

She was breathing hard even before he dragged her back round to cover her mouth with his. She was lost even as, still kissing her, he discarded his jeans, letting them lie where they fell. She surrendered willingly as he pulled her down on the bed with him and, pleasuring her with his hands and mouth, drew off the rest of her clothing.

Dee wanted it all until the very last moment when he was poised above her, handsome face set, body hard with bone and muscle. That was when fear suddenly gripped her—she knew she would never come back from this point a whole person. But it was already too late; he was penetrating her, heart, body, soul, and she was riven, contracting, crying out more in shock than pain.

Then a hand was stroking her hair, a voice caressing her with words. 'It's okay… It's okay… I won't hurt you…I'll never hurt you…I love you…'

Dee barely registered it as he kissed her lips, her face, her hair, making desire kick in her belly once more until her legs uncoiled and he began to move inside her, fragmenting all thought.

For a moment she lay passive beneath him, impaled by the sheer force of it, then passion and love fused and she reached for him, clung to him, moaning aloud as she rose to each powerful thrust of his body, accepting him into the depth of her own till pleasure was sweet agony and they were one, drowning, crying, dying in it.

It was a perfect act of union. Baxter was driven by an urge so primitive he forgot a lifetime's caution and cried out her name as he spilled his seed into her. Then, spent, he rolled with her clasped in his arms.

Dee lay with her head against his thundering heart, and struggled to calm the beat of her own. She'd never been with another man, never made love before, but she knew instinctively that it would not be like this. No one else would reach her this way.

Her certainty of it was absolute. Her first lover, Baxter Ross, was also her ultimate, even if a legion were to follow. She would never be complete without him—a sobering realisation when taken with the fact that happy-ever-afters weren't on his agenda.

He tilted her head back, his smile fading at her solemn face. 'All right?'

Dee nodded, but it was a lie. She wasn't all right. How could she be? Her life had just changed for ever.

Not his, of course. He'd done this before. Probably a thousand times. It was a thought she could have done without.

'Something's wrong. Tell me.' He watched her changing expression.

Dee shook her head and, slipping from under his arm, clutched a sheet to hide her nakedness.

'Nothing's wrong.' She tried to sound tough and uncaring, but she heard the cracks in her voice. In a moment she would be crying, betraying her real feelings. 'I have to go.'

She edged to one side of the bed and picked up her discarded T-shirt; it effectively covered her from neck to thigh. But, before she could put on her jeans, he stretched out an arm and pulled her round.

'*Go?*' His eyes expressed disbelief.

What did he expect? That she would cling to him?

'Go where?'

Dee had no idea. Anywhere. Just so long as he wasn't there to see her break down.

'*I have to go,*' she repeated, and, desperation giving her strength, she slipped free of his grip.

She didn't hang around. She snatched her pants and jeans from the floor and, ignoring his command to stop, rushed to the door.

It was absurd, of course, to think she could just run away. She reached the first landing, then paused to drag on her jeans and appreciate the fact she'd left her shoes upstairs. Pride wouldn't let her return for them; practicality told her she wouldn't get far barefoot and in the dark. She slumped down at the top of the next flight of stairs.

That was where Baxter found her, having hung around long enough to pull on his own trousers. He sat beside her on the cold step. She didn't look at him. He sensed her fragility, and didn't try to touch her.

'Is it what I said earlier?' he asked her quietly. 'About loving you? Is that what's scaring you?'

Dee shook her head. She wondered if it was scaring *him*—that she might have taken him seriously.

'Because you don't have to love me, you know,' he continued in the same vein. 'I accept that. Just stay a while.'

Confused, Dee turned to stare at him. 'Stay the night, you mean?'

'A night, a week, a month, a year.' He seemed to be saying it was up to her.

Dee didn't think so. If it was her choice, there would be no talk of time limits. And how much harder would it be to leave in a week, a month, a year?

She found the strength now. 'I can't stay.'

He didn't seem to hear as he brushed a strand of hair from her cold cheek and kissed her gently. 'Stay and let me take care of you.'

Sweet words, but they broke the spell for Dee. She'd heard them before from another man, and they brought back such bad memories that she knocked his hand away.

'I am *not a child*,' she raged back at him. 'And if I wanted *taking care of,* I could have stayed at home and let my stepfather do it… As in, do *it*.' Her mouth twisted, revealing the stark, bitter truth.

Baxter reeled from it, any jealousy he'd felt for Edward Litton turning into revulsion. No wonder she had run from home.

But was he any better? He had always known she was vulnerable, had had from the start an urge to protect her, but there were other feelings for her he couldn't control.

'What have I done?' He looked into eyes that were feral with distrust. 'If I'd known… I thought if I made love to you—'

'I'd be easy?' Dee cut in, angry with herself now. 'Well,

you were right, I was, so spare us the guilt trip. You wanted me, I wanted you. We had each other. End of story.'

She rose before he could stop her, and retraced her steps to the bedroom, meaning to collect her shoes and go.

He was there in the doorway when she turned.

'So just tell me. What was it about, Dee?' he asked, struggling with some emotion. 'Curiosity? A game? Or some kind of pay-back for what Litton did?'

Dee shook her head. 'I don't know what you're talking about.'

'Don't you? You wait till I'm on my knees to you then walk away.' He made it sound as if it had been some grand plan on her part.

'*Edward* has nothing to do with this!' she denied, temper rising once again.'You think I ever let him touch me? Reach me? Make love to me?'

'So why let *me?*' he countered. 'If you don't want any kind of relationship?'

Dee thought the answer was painfully obvious, and confessing wouldn't make it hurt less. She settled for a shrug that he could interpret how he liked.

His mouth went into a tight white line. 'I could have made you pregnant, you know. Have you considered that?'

Dee hadn't, but he clearly had. 'So that's what's bothering you.'

'Of course it's bothering me!' he exploded at her apparent indifference. 'If you're pregnant, it'll be my responsibility as well as yours.'

'Fine. Great. Let's get married now just in case.' The suggestion was purely sarcastic, a throwaway line as she made to walk past him.

He caught her arm and held her there by his side, his voice harsh as he replied, 'Okay, let's.'

'Very funny.' Dee assumed he was trying to be, but there wasn't a flicker of amusement on his hard, handsome face. 'I was joking.'

'I know,' he told her. 'I wasn't.'

He really was offering to marry her—had he just missed the last ten years of social development?

'People don't marry these days because they're pregnant,' she informed him stonily.

'I do.' He didn't care what other people did.

'You're crazy,' Dee accused, even as she reflected on her own sanity.

She loved this man. He was prepared to marry her. Why was she talking him out of it?

'It's not a good enough reason,' she reminded them both.

'You want others?'

'Yes.'

'All right. We've just had the most incredible sex,' he stated with jaw-dropping frankness. 'You may not be aware of that, being new to the whole thing, but take my word for it.'

Well, Dee thought, she *had* asked! She blushed to the roots of her hair, but didn't pull away as he drew her round to face him.

'Add to that the fact we're surprisingly compatible,' he ran on, 'in intellect, interests and attitudes. Having had a number of failed relationships, I can testify to the importance of such a symbiosis.'

'*Symbiosis?*' Dee wasn't quite sure what it meant, but was unable to resist a dry, 'You really know how to romance a girl, Doc.'

'I've already tried the romance angle,' he pointed out. 'It didn't get me very far, remember?'

Actually, Dee didn't. 'I think I must have missed that part.'

'Then let me recap for you.' His mouth slanted with self-mockery. 'I tell you I love you and ask you to stay with me. You tell me to get lost, and stamp off up here to get the rest of your things... Forgive me if I thought a different approach was called for,' he concluded, matching her sarcasm.

But Dee didn't hear it. She hadn't got further than the love part.

'You love me?' she echoed, staring at him.

He gave her an impatient look. 'I've said so often enough.'

She shook her head. No, he hadn't. It wasn't the kind of thing she would forget.

'Just once,' she corrected, 'when we were making love.'

'Okay, once then,' he conceded. 'Isn't that enough?'

She agreed that it might have been in different circumstances. 'I imagine men say all sorts of things in the throes of passion.'

'Some men,' he qualified. 'Not me.'

No, not him. Baxter Ross only ever said what he meant. She knew that. How had she forgotten it?

She was torn between laughing and crying. She was such a fool.

'Do you want me to say it again?' He was clearly reluctant.

But now Dee understood. He had his pride, just as she had hers. If they weren't careful, they'd lose everything to it.

'No, I think it's my turn.' Steady blue eyes met the blue-grey of his, and in her gaze was all the things she wanted to say. She still gave him the words, lifting her mouth to whisper against his, 'I love you, Baxter Ross, and that's what scares me. You say stay "a while". I love you so much I couldn't bear just a day or a week or a—'

The rest was lost as he drew her into his arms and stole the breath from her in a kiss that spoke of a love as real as her own.

When he finally raised his head, it was to demand, 'You think I'm ever going to let you go? After what you've put me through?'

'What *I've* put *you* through?' Dee had to protest.

'Quite! Like that night at Cat's? One moment we're in bed together and I'm feeling like the luckiest guy on earth—' he smiled at the memory, then grimaced at what followed '—the next you're announcing your engagement to Joseph and I'm out in the cold.'

'There was nothing between Joseph and I,' Dee repeated for what seemed like the hundredth time.

'Yes, all right. On a logical level, I knew it,' he admitted. 'On a logical level, I even admired your altruism. I just had visions of making a fool of myself at the wedding.'

'I assumed you wouldn't go,' Dee revealed. 'But Cat said you would. According to her, you have masochistic tendencies.'

'Yes, well, if I have—' he gave an expressive sigh '—it hasn't stopped her feeding them over the last few weeks... It's been Dee this, Dee that. What a great girl you are. What a wonderful mother you'd make. How clever, talented, beautiful et cetera, et cetera... No one can ever accuse my sister of subtlety.'

Dee laughed, saying half seriously, 'I'm surprised it didn't put you off.'

'What—as well as making me feel like some ageing Lothario to your sweet young thing?' A pointed glance reminded her who had originally made him feel that way.

'I was never sweet,' she protested.

'No,' he agreed. 'If anything, you're rather tough.'

Dee didn't take it as an insult. It seemed important that he saw her for who she was.

'So where do we go from here?' A hand lifted to caress the nape of her neck, and her bones turned fluid once more.

Dee no longer wanted to go anywhere. 'I'll stay, if that's what you want.'

'You know it is.' He bent to kiss her softly on the lips, before adding, 'But I'd prefer a formalised arrangement.'

Dee smiled quizzically. 'I'm not sure what you mean.'

'I'd like you to marry me,' he said, in plainer English.

'If I'm pregnant?'

'No, in either case.'

He spoke so matter-of-factly Dee didn't know how to react. Could he really want to marry her?

'I'm not doing this very well, am I?' he continued, at her silence. 'I should go down on one knee, I suppose.'

A wry look appeared on Dee's face at the idea of Baxter Ross so humble. 'I'd rather you didn't.'

'Is that a yes or a no?'

'More an "are we crazy?".'

'Possibly,' he conceded, but he was smiling as he scented victory. 'Register office or the full works?'

'I haven't said yes, yet,' she pointed out.

'Okay, we'll sleep on it,' he suggested, already drawing her back towards the bed.

'*Sleep?*'

'What else?'

'I can't imagine,' she laughed back, even as he pulled the T-shirt loose from her jeans and began to set an all-time speed record for undressing another human being.

They made love the same way, with an urgency to be part of each other once more, then slept, their bodies entwined, until desire stirred with the first light of dawn.

They were married a month later in the church where the Ross family had had their weddings and christenings for the last four generations. In time to come Baxter would maintain he'd dragged Dee kicking and screaming to the altar—and it was partly true. She'd believed in Baxter and her love for him, but she still hadn't believed in marriage—until the moment she floated up the aisle in white satin, and he turned to gaze at her, a smile slanting that absurdly handsome face.

It was then she saw the future stretching before them—years of loving and laughing, babies and battles, good times and bad. But always together, from this life to the next—soul mates who'd found each other.

PARTY TIME!

How would you like to win a year's supply of Mills & Boon® Books? Well, you can and they're FREE! Simply complete the competition below and send it to us by 31st August 1998. The first five correct entries picked after the closing date will each win a year's subscription to the Mills & Boon series of their choice. What could be easier?

BALLOONS	BUFFET	ENTERTAIN
STREAMER	DANCING	INVITE
DRINKS	CELEBRATE	FANCY DRESS
MUSIC	PARTIES	HANGOVER

S	O	E	T	A	R	B	E	L	E	C
T	E	F	M	U	S	I	C	D	D	H
S	U	I	V	Z	T	E	Y	R	A	A
N	E	N	T	E	R	T	A	I	N	N
O	B	V	E	R	E	H	K	N	C	G
O	J	I	F	O	A	L	R	K	I	O
L	M	T	F	V	M	P	U	S	N	V
L	P	E	U	Q	E	N	Z	S	G	E
A	W	G	B	X	R	C	T	B	Y	R
B	F	A	N	C	Y	D	R	E	S	S

C8B

Please turn over for details of how to enter...

HOW TO ENTER

Can you find our twelve party words? They're all hidden somewhere in the grid. They can be read backwards, forwards, up, down or diagonally. As you find each word in the grid put a line through it. When you have completed your wordsearch, don't forget to fill in the coupon below, pop this page into an envelope and post it today—you don't even need a stamp!

Mills & Boon Party Time! Competition
FREEPOST CN81, Croydon, Surrey, CR9 3WZ
EIRE readers send competition to PO Box 4546, Dublin 24.

Please tick the series you would like to receive if you are one of the lucky winners

Presents™ ❑ Enchanted™ ❑ Medical Romance™ ❑
Historical Romance™ ❑ Temptation® ❑

Are you a Reader Service™ Subscriber?   Yes ❑   No ❑

Mrs/Ms/Miss/Mr ....Intials ....
(BLOCK CAPITALS PLEASE)

Surname...

Address ....

....

....Postcode..........................

(I am over 18 years of age)   C8B

One application per household. Competition open to residents of the UK and Ireland only. You may be mailed with offers from other reputable companies as a result of this application. If you would prefer not to receive such offers, please tick box. ❑

Closing date for entries is 31st August 1998.

Mills & Boon® is a registered trademark of Harlequin Mills & Boon Limited.

MILLS & BOON®

Next Month's Romances

Each month you can choose from a wide variety of romance novels from Mills & Boon. Below are the new titles to look out for next month from the Presents™ and Enchanted™ series.

Presents™

THE DIAMOND BRIDE	Carole Mortimer
THE SHEIKH'S SEDUCTION	Emma Darcy
THE SEDUCTION PROJECT	Miranda Lee
THE UNMARRIED HUSBAND	Cathy Williams
THE TEMPTATION GAME	Kate Walker
THE GROOM'S DAUGHTER	Natalie Fox
HIS PERFECT WIFE	Susanne McCarthy
A FORBIDDEN MARRIAGE	Margaret Mayo

Enchanted™

BABY IN A MILLION	Rebecca Winters
MAKE BELIEVE ENGAGEMENT	Day Leclaire
THE WEDDING PROMISE	Grace Green
A MARRIAGE WORTH KEEPING	Kate Denton
TRIAL ENGAGEMENT	Barbara McMahon
ALMOST A FATHER	Pamela Bauer & Judy Kaye
MARRIED BY MISTAKE!	Renee Roszel
THE TENDERFOOT	Patricia Knoll

H1 9802

Available from WH Smith, John Menzies, Martins, Tesco and Asda

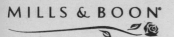

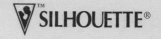